An (Un)Helpful Guide to Writing a Novel

Dawn Vogel

CONTENTS

ACKNOWLEDGEMENTS

This book would not exist if not for an exchange in the early days of BlueSky with a fellow author named George Penney. Our back and forth about what books about writing novels really needed had me scribbling an outline on post-it notes and laughing about the idea. But then I wrote it. Thank you immensely, George!

The other person involved heavily in this book was Torrey Podmajersky, who read the revised draft. She also pointed out my excess of exclamation points and told me a book like this was required to have illustrations. And because Torrey is a font of brilliant ideas, she was absolutely right.

(Because I am not a very good artist, the illustrations might look like they were drawn by a five-year-old. I assure you that I have not been a five-year-old for a very long time. But I like to think their "quality" adds a level of charm. Also, because Torrey suggested them, she got an illustration of her, which you'll find in Chapter 3.)

Finally, the title of this book is a nod to a phenomenon in which K-pop fans make "(un)helpful" guides to the members of a given K-pop group. They are really quite helpful when you're trying to differentiate between the members of groups and learn a few quirks to remember those members by. And since my husband, Jeremy Zimmerman, is responsible for turning me into a K-pop multi-stan and suggesting the title for this book, he also gets thanks here.

INTRODUCTION

There are a lot of books that are supposed to tell you how to write a novel. They focus on things like character arcs and genre expectations and how to get from point A to point B.

This isn't one of them.

Personally, I hate writing novels. And yet, since 2008, I've written and published a trilogy of novels and a stand-alone novel, and I've written a bunch of novellas and a bunch of failed (incomplete) novels.

It might not be so much that I hate writing novels, but I find them much more difficult to write than short fiction. With short fiction, you can generally draft a story, revise it, and start sending it out into the world in short order. With novels, you write for a longer amount of time, then you revise, revise some more, revise a little more, maybe revise some more ... it's a long process.

So why am I writing a book about how to write a novel when I hate this process?

This book is for people like me. Sort of. It collects some of the tips and tricks I've found helpful when I do sit down to write a novel. But it also acknowledges the difficulty of writing a novel in a world where most of us can't be full-time writers for whatever reason. It looks at aspects of time management and human management, for writers who have disabilities or other factors that make more conventional writing advice unhelpful.

And it injects a whole lot of humor into what can otherwise be a somewhat humorless proposition.

So I hope you'll find this book useful. And even if you don't find it useful, I hope you will be entertained.

Because the writing world needs more entertainment.

~

I suppose I should tell you a little about myself.

I taught myself to read at age three, and I wrote my first story a year or two later. My mom had to type it for me. It was about what you'd expect out of a four or five year old.

I kept writing, either by hand or typing it myself. These are all top secret, never to be shared, stories. Mostly self-insert fiction of a teenage girl who was absolutely the coolest and the cutest. Trust me, no one needs to read those stories.

But then I met my now husband, and he introduced me to the world of writing stories that other people paid money for (what?) and NaNoWriMo—National Novel Writing Month.[1] This seemed awesome, so I started writing stories and getting paid for it, and also attempting novels.

Fast-forward fifteen-ish years, and here I am, author of a whole lot of published words. Some of them were published by people who paid me money for them. Some of them were self-published. I write for adults, teens, pre-teens, small children, and anyone else who wants to read what I wrote. (Though I'm not sure who I've missed in the above list. Animals? Aliens? Who knows.)

I'm also an editor of non-fiction as my day job, and while fiction and non-fiction are incredibly different beasts, there's a lot in common between any editing and any writing. Mostly, it's

---

[1] More on this in Chapter 1.

commas. No matter which you're doing, you always have to deal with the pesky commas, literally the most complex piece of punctuation in the English language.

It's okay. I like commas.

What else about me? I'm a geek and a nerd, a crafter, and a cat mom. (I love my human nieces and nephews and am very glad they live with humans who are not me.) I sing (decently), I dance (badly), and I have acted (mediocrely), so I'm at least a one-and-a-half threat.

And I like laughing and making people around me laugh. So that explains a whole lot of what you've read so far, and what's still to come.

~

The Year of Not Writing Novels

In 2022, I made the decision to take a year off from writing novels after fourteen years of on and off novel writing. I made my decision after a pair of online courses, one on creativity and one on setting goals and making plans. They both got me thinking about what I do, why I do it, and what I want out of it.

The shortest possible version is: I love to write. However, the more I write, the more I gravitate toward certain lengths. And the length I don't love is the novel. Novels take me longer than I would like to outline, draft, and revise. And while there's a brief spike of accomplishment at various parts of the process, they ultimately tend to have more of a dragging-down effect on me.

And I'm not going to lie. While rejections on shorter pieces sting, it's usually a quick and temporary sting. Querying novels and receiving rejections from agents is a much stronger sting for me. The process is complicated, tedious, and often fraught with disappointment. And I possibly dislike the querying process more than I dislike actually writing the novel that leads to querying.

Throughout 2022, which I dubbed the Year of Not Writing Novels, I did periodic check-ins with my feelings. I anticipated I might realize I had a novel I really wanted to write, something worth putting in the time and effort. At three months, I was completely happy with my decision, as I felt a lot less overwhelmed with balancing a novel project with my other writing. It meant I could bounce around between shorter projects without feeling like I was neglecting my longer projects.

But by six months out from my decision, I found an idea I thought was worth exploring as a novella, if not a full-length novel.[2] I spent July working on that novella, and I wound up with a completed draft.

But then I had to revise it, and I found, yet again, the project I had been so excited about was now a burden. I did some more research related to it, figured out some tweaks to make to it, and promptly fizzled out on the idea. There were chunks of the book that needed to be entirely rewritten to turn it into the vision I had in my mind. But I couldn't muster the enthusiasm I needed for doing the work. I spent most of November 2022 trying to make headway on rewriting and revising, and ultimately wrote about 1,000 new words in two early scenes. And that was it.

So by the end of the Year of Not Writing Novels, I came to the conclusion that I'd made the right decision. I knew I could continue to revisit my decision, and maybe someday I would go back to that novella or any of the other partially imagined novels I have kicking around in my head.

Since that time, I haven't had any huge new ideas, though I plotted out a new novella and wrote it (at the same time I was drafting this book, in fact). I planned to give myself a lot of time to spend on it, but the words flooded out. I know it requires a lot of revisions, but I'm not rushing it. Sometimes, slow but steady wins the race.

~

---

[2] Generally speaking, a novel is at least 40,000 words, though most novels you've read are probably closer to a minimum of 75,000 words. A novella is between 17,500 and 40,000 words. You've also got novelettes from around 8,000 to 17,500 words, and short stories from roughly 1,000 words to 8,000 words. There's often some wiggle room in the definitions of these, depending on who you ask.

What This Book Is and Isn't

Though I'm a prolific writer and an experienced editor of fiction and non-fiction, I'm not going to talk a lot about the finer points of how to write in this book. There are many, many books in the world that can tell you how to write.

In my personal experience, the best way to learn to write is to do it. Write a lot. Write horribly. Write beautifully. You learn from every word you put on the page, whether you want to publish those words or hide them away in your sock drawer. (Suggestion: get a bigger sock drawer if that's your plan, or you'll run out of room for the socks.)

What this book is meant to be is recommendations for some approaches to writing a novel that might work for you. And because everyone is different, not all the recommendations will fit every reader or writer. There are lived experiences I cannot address because they aren't my lived experiences. But I hope every reader of this book will take away at least one piece of advice that resonates for them and helps them write the novel of their dreams. That's all I can ask for.

That being said, I have read and synthesized a lot of writing advice, so some of it is naturally going to come through in what I write here. There's a lot of writing advice out there in the world, and while there's plenty of reiterating what's been said dozens of times before, you may also come across some new-to-you pieces of advice.

The trick is to find the pieces of advice that resonate with you (and this is the most important factor—*only grabbing the bits that resonate with you*) and synthesizing those new pieces into your personal system. For me, when I'm reading writing advice, that looks like sitting down with my own system and seeing where the things that strike me as useful can be merged into my larger system.

Some of the pieces will slot in nicely, as they're using different vocabulary or suggesting an alternative way to think about something you already do. But other pieces might wind up seeming like they go to a different puzzle than the one you're working on. So those might need to be set aside for the time being, and revisited once you've got the basic system pieces all put together.

But it's also important to remember that if a piece of writing advice doesn't work for you, you don't have to use it. Writing advice should be approached more like writing suggestions, not The Law.

Because when it comes down to it, the only real Law of writing is you have to get the words on paper (virtual or otherwise) if you want anyone to read them. So whatever it takes for you to get those words is valid. (But you shouldn't steal them from other people. That's bad.[3])

~

This book is divided into three chapters. The first and longest chapter is "How to Write a Novel." It offers some suggestions for getting started, keeping going, and what to do after you've finished your novel. It also has some overall tips for how to juggle novel writing with other parts of your life.

The second chapter is "Excuses: How Your Novel Can't Possibly Get Written," where I talk more about the many, many distractions and other things that get in the way of writing and finishing. There may be some sage advice for how to cope with these things. There will also be a lot more discussion about accepting those things we cannot change, but, like, not in a self-help book sort of way.

The third chapter is "How to Trick Yourself into Writing a Novel," which covers the ways in which you can use rewards and gamification to motivate yourself to get the writing done. I've got

---

[3] It's also worth noting that in my opinion, which is also the opinion of many authors and editors, using artificial intelligence (AI) or large language models (LLM) or other forms of machine-based writing counts as stealing other peoples' words. Those models are, for the most part, trained on copyrighted materials the programmers do not have the legal rights to use for this purpose. So yeah, that counts as stealing in my book. And to be completely honest, most of what they're going to churn out as "writing" is not good. You're better off writing your own stuff. Promise. (There are forms of AI/LLM/etc. that can be used for checking spelling, grammar, sentence structure, etc., and those are not cheating. However, they present their own issues, which I'll talk about in the section on editing in Chapter 1.)

suggestions for things you can do that cost zero dollars and things you can do if you have a little money to spend. I crowdsourced a lot of the ideas in this chapter, so some things are specific, while others are broader categories. But those specific things may remind you of something you personally can use as motivation that I haven't mentioned.

None of these chapters are comprehensive, but perhaps the ideas and suggestions I present will give you more ideas on how to make the novel writing process, including the distractions and the rewards, work for you. Like I said, read my suggestions, see what resonates with you, and integrate them into your personal system.

And let the words flow!

CHAPTER ONE: HOW TO WRITE A NOVEL

So, you want to write a novel.

Or you're on the fence about writing a novel.

If you've already decided, cool. You can skip ahead a bit if you want to, since I'm going to talk the tentative novelist through making a decision first. (But if you're second guessing yourself because you just read the Introduction, and now you're worried you're also going to hate writing a novel, stick around.)

For those on the fence, I'm going to be honest. Writing a novel is work. There may be times when the words fly from your fingers, but there will also be times when the words "he said," "she said," or "they said" seem fraught.

But.

You can do it.

Every novelist was once an aspiring novelist. They all had to start somewhere. Even if you don't think of yourself as a writer, if you write, you become a writer. (Spoiler alert: you don't even have to be published. The act of writing makes you a writer.)

Even if you write a novel and decide it should never see the light of day or be read by any other person in the world, getting to the point where you type "The End" is a huge accomplishment.

And you might figure out that you like writing novels, and you've made the right decision. Not everyone is like me.

So go ahead and give it a shot.

~

Butt in Chair, Words on Page, or What You Really Need for a Novel: Ideas and Time

Now, back to the opening of this chapter. So, you want to write a novel.

In my experience, you need two things to write a novel. Ideas and time. Or, as some people say, "butt in chair, words on page."

This first section of the chapter is going to talk about ideas. After that, I'll talk about the time part of the equation. Along the way, I'll share a few thoughts about outlining and outlines, which can be useful to novel writing (though not everyone agrees on that).

So here we go!

~

Ideas

In order to get started, you're going to need an idea.

If you're anything like me, your mind just went completely blank. No thoughts, no ideas.

Hopefully, in this case, you're not like me. After all, you're reading this book, which suggests you have an idea for a novel, and you just need to figure out how to do it.

But perhaps you're thinking, "I have an idea, but ..."

1. "I don't know how to write a novel."
2. "I'm not sure what to do with it."
3. "I'm not sure it's enough of an idea."
4. "I'm not sure if it's too much of an idea."
5. "I'm not sure which idea to start with."
6. "Nope, no ideas."

All of these answers (or things that sound similar to one of them) are fine, because I've got something to say about each of them. For the first answer, well, you've come to entirely the right place, which is this whole book. For the remaining five answers, you'll find sections following this one where I answer each of them, roughly in order.

If your answer isn't on the above list, don't panic. More likely than not, your answer is related to one of these, and you'll find a section below that you realize is what you were trying to say in your answer.

Now, if your answer was something like "42" or "purple," I don't know if I can help you much. And if your answer was something like "why?", that's not actually an answer, it's another question, and that's more existential than I'm prepared to answer in the scope of this book. Sorry.

~

Developing Your Ideas

If you've got an idea but you don't know what to do with it, that might suggest it needs more development before it's ready for you to start writing. There are tons of different ways you can develop your ideas. Doing some of these things can also help make it easier to draft your novel. These include prewriting, brain dumping, and rubber ducking.

Prewriting:
How many times have you been working on a writing project, only to have to stop to figure out some tiny detail, without which you can't go forward?

There are some authors and advice-givers who say, "go forward anyway, and figure it out later." And that makes sense for some details. But here, I'm talking more about the "this is not something I can gloss over because it informs what comes next" types of details.

Prewriting can be part of this process. It can involve things like **free writing**, *making lists*, or *iterating on ideas*, which I'll discuss in that order.

Free writing is, in a sense, writing without plans to use what you've written as part of the project you're working on. Maybe you've got two characters who are polar opposites and who would have the worst time collaborating. And maybe throwing them together in a scene where they must collaborate will let you write something that could be explosive or could let the characters see one another in a different light. You might also discover the characters have more in common than you previously realized. While your novel may not call for a scene in which these characters work together, you can learn a lot about them in this sort of free-writing exercise.

Another way free writing can work well for novelists is to set a timer and start writing **about** your plot or any sticking points you're running into. You're not writing something that is in the novel itself. Think of it more like an email to a friend where you're trying to tell them about your idea. Getting yourself to write about the topic for five or ten minutes and trying to not stop writing the whole time can get your brain loosened up to find solutions to problems. I like to use this sort of free writing when I'm working on a piece involving an element of mystery, because as the author, I need to know an awful lot about the details of the mystery. Free writing about the mystery lets me get a bunch of ideas out, which I can then sift through later to inform my story. Maybe not everything I write will be useful for the truth of what happened, but then some of those discarded bits might become useful-to-the-mystery-story red herrings. (For some people, this is also brain dumping, which I talk about more below.)

Making lists is a form of prewriting I do for some projects, though I don't always remember to make the right lists. When I was writing *Promise Me Nothing*, I ran into a problem that could have been solved with some prewriting work, specifically in the form of making lists. The novel takes place in a school, and while I had lists of teachers and students and classes, I had never put those together. This left me scrambling to determine which teacher taught which class, and which other students were in that class, as those things would color my protagonist's thoughts about her daily routine.

I wound up taking some time to sort out a bunch of these details, making yet another list, and it made writing the remainder of the novel a whole lot easier. I could refer to the class schedule, with teachers and other students in each class, and then write the scenes where something in those classes impacted my protagonist.

Sometimes I found new ideas for how to shape a scene when I realized there was an interesting combination of students, whether in terms of their personalities or their supernatural powers. *Iterating on ideas* can take many forms. You might do a free-writing exercise, note what elements come up frequently, and then do a second free-writing exercise focused on those elements. Your lists might spawn other lists. You might try some form of idea mapping based on what you've come up with previously. This form of pre-writing is also related to the next topic, brain dumping.

Brain Dumping:
Sometimes when I'm starting a story or novel, I have a clear picture of what it will look like. But other times, I have vague ideas, and I need to do a bit of brainstorming in order to get to a point where I can start writing. In some cases, this involves brain dumping, too.

Whereas brainstorming is thinking of ideas, brain dumping, for me, is a form of prewriting where I write (type, more often) what I know about the story—every little bit of it. This can include characters, historical or scientific facts, specific themes I'd like the story to focus on, and more. And then, as I organize and refine that information, I get to the brainstorming part, where I find the connections in what I have and flesh them out a bit more with "what ifs" and "maybes."

When it comes to brain dumping for a novel, you might find that pen and paper are more useful to you, or you might choose to use a digital document of some sort. I tend to like the latter because I can easily copy and paste links to online sources I find and can pull some quotes from those same sources relevant to my plans. And because brain dumping for a novel might involve a lot of information, it can be nice to have it all in a single document, which I can then reorganize, color code, or whatever else I need to do to get all the pieces in a format where I can then use them to write a novel.

Some of what I come up with during a brain dump/storm won't make it into the final product, because as I work through the directions those ideas point to, I find problems with them or decide a different direction is more interesting to me. I try to keep track of what I've thought about and discarded too, though, so I don't wind up in the same place a few minutes, hours, days, or weeks later.

17

Using this brain-dumping technique takes up some of my writing time, but by getting things sorted out at the beginning, rather than midway through when I've realized I have no idea what I'm doing, I end up saving time later. It's got similarities to outlining, but it feels organic enough that I think people who are allergic to outlining might find some use in brain dumping as well.

Rubber Ducking:

Say what?

Rubber ducking comes from the computer programming world. It's typically known as "rubber duck debugging" there, as it's what a programmer might use when trying to determine why their code isn't doing what they expect or want it to do. In this method, they explain each line of the code to their rubber duck (real or imaginary). As they talk through what each line of the code should be doing, they're likely to catch the errors that prevent their code from working.

I prefer calling it rubber ducking because it's kind of hilarious to say, and because most authors aren't debugging their writing ...

Or are they?

While the idea of talking to a rubber duck might seem strange, it can also be a good tool for authors, when you've reached a point in a story you can't get beyond. By breaking down your story and talking yourself through it (with or without the assistance of an inanimate object), you may be able to find the place where things go awry and figure out how to fix it.

If you're fortunate enough to live with another person who will listen to you while you talk through story problems, you don't necessarily need a rubber duck. One thing I've found, however, is many authors want their person to listen and perhaps ask questions, but they may not want them to offer solutions. Your mileage may vary on this aspect--some authors prefer if their person tosses out ideas, too, no matter how bizarre they might be, because it could get the author's brain pointed in a different, helpful direction. I alternate between the two options, personally, but I let my person (my husband) know if I would like questions or answers when I launch into a story discussion with him.

But if you want a sounding board that won't respond at all, you could talk to a pet, a piece of furniture, or, if you have one, a rubber duck.

It's important to recognize that it's okay to not have every detail of your idea developed in your first draft. That's incredibly normal, and even experienced novelists often realize they need to tweak something in their draft to work with the ending, or the middle, or some other portion. It's fine to not be sure you've got ALL the "right" details related to your idea when you're starting out writing a novel, whether it's your first or tenth or hundredth. Just write it, then figure out the details during the revisions process.

~

The Size of an Idea (Warning, Contains Math)

How do you figure out whether your idea is a short story, a novel, or something else entirely?

Sometimes, it's easy to figure out. Some ideas have a large enough scope that you know from the get-go they're going to be something as long as a novel, or maybe even a series. But sometimes, you have an idea you think can be self-contained as a short story, and then it spirals into something bigger. Or you finish the short story you wanted to tell, and everyone who reads it thinks it's meant to be something bigger. (And sometimes, you turn that short story into a novel, and then someone asks you if there's more adventures set in that world. Or if the robot will be okay. And then you realize your short story was a trilogy in disguise.)

Learning how to evaluate your ideas for size is a process. Even after writing for fifteen years, sometimes my ideas trick me into thinking they'll be something short and easy. And then suddenly I'm plotting multiple plot threads and subplots and character arcs.

And if I was planning to write something short for a specific reason, that means I'm back to the drawing board for a new idea for whatever that specific reason was.

While it's not always easy to distinguish between the ideas that will become a short story and those that will become a novel or series at first, this is one of the places where I find outlining can be a huge help. If I start plotting out a story and realize it's got more than half a dozen scenes, it's probably not actually a short story. Likewise, if I'm trying to plot out a novel idea and can't get past Chapter 5 or so, that's a sign that there's not enough of an idea to sustain it as a novel.

Looking at the number of plot threads, subplots, characters, and locations can also often help you estimate the length of a given piece. For most short stories, you probably have one main plot thread and maybe a subplot, along with a handful of characters, and maybe a location or two. As you add more plot threads, subplots, characters, and locations, you should expect the size of the project will grow.

Sometimes, too, you have a piece you think is complete, but other people want to know what happens next. And that can be both frustrating and exciting. It's frustrating because you've worked hard to write something and thought you were done, and then you find out you're not. But it's exciting, because if people want more, that generally means you're off to a great start. You've hooked them with your writing. As one of my friends often asked when we were telling a story together through gaming, "And then what happens?" There's not much greater than that.

But we can also apply some math to this question. If you are not a math fan, bear with me. I'm making this as non-math fan friendly as I can, because I, too, am not much of a math fan.[1]

Orson Scott Card came up with something called the MICE Quotient, which was then expanded upon and turned into an actual mathematical equation by Mary Robinette Kowal, though other authors have also talked about a similar or comparable equation.

---

[1] True fact: I picked my major in college based on what required only easy math classes. At the same time, I can do a lot of calculations in my head, so I'm apparently not a HARD math fan.

You can read about the MICE Quotient and MICE Equation online or listen to authors talk about it on many podcasts, but I'll summarize it, how it works, and the equation that comes from it. "MICE" stands for Milieu, Idea, Character, and Event, and Orson Scott Card used it primarily to categorize types of stories. Milieu is another word for setting and means stories focused on the setting or the world, often with a character or characters journeying to a new place different from their home. Idea stories are often mysteries, because they ask a question and then answer that question by the end. Character stories are about character growth and change, while Event stories are about (unsurprisingly) an event, where the characters must then deal with the aftermath.

A story can be more than one of these types. Authors are often told to have their characters grow and change, so many novels are Character stories. But those characters might grow and change by going somewhere (Milieu stories), answering a question (Idea stories), or dealing with an event (Event stories). And perhaps those characters are confronted with an event, need to go somewhere else, and then answer a question (making it also an Event, Milieu, and Idea story, respectively).

For those stories that include multiple story types, the recommendation is to "nest" the elements like a matryoshka—a set of nesting dolls, in which each doll opens to reveal a smaller doll (until the tiniest doll, which doesn't open). The idea is that whatever you open first, you close last.[2] So in a character-driven mystery story (Character and Idea), you could open with the character or the mystery, then introduce the second. But as you close out the story, you'd want to conclude the second element first, and the first element second.

---

[2] If you're familiar with HTML coding and nesting elements within, that's another metaphor that's useful here. If you're not a coder, don't worry about it. The nesting dolls have your back.

In the metaphor of the matryoshka, if you've opened up all of them, all the way to the tiny, non-opening doll, you can't close the largest nesting doll first, because then all the smaller nesting dolls are trapped outside. You open them one at a time, in size order, to be able to look at all of them, and close them in the opposite order to put them away.

So, if I started with the character and then introduced the mystery, I would close out the mystery arc before I closed out the character arc. If I started with the mystery arc and then tossed in the character arc, I'd want to wrap the character arc first and then the mystery arc at the end.

Where the equation portion comes into play is more related to story length, or the size of your idea. (If you hate math, now is the time to hang on to your hat, or socks, or whatever. I'll explain it in a less-mathy way in a moment.)

The equation is a complex one that looks like this:

$$L = (((C+P)*750)*M)/1.5$$

L is length. C is characters. P is places. M is MICE quotient elements.

Getting back to high school algebra order of operations, you add together your number of characters (C) and number of places where the piece will be set (P). You multiply that by 750, which is the presumption of about how many words you'll need to adequately cover each character and place. Then you multiply that number by the number of MICE Quotient elements (M). And then you divide that number by 1.5, which reflects the overlap between the various elements and means your story won't be quite as long as the initial equation suggests.

So, if I'm writing a story involving 5 characters who will go to 5 different locations, that equals 10 for the first part of the equation. Multiplying that number by 750 gives me 7,500. Then, using the earlier example of a character-driven mystery, that gives me a MICE quotient of 2, which I multiply with 7,500 to get 15,000. And then I divide that by 1.5, giving me 10,000. So arguably, that story would probably wind up around 10,000 words, or at least in that ballpark.

If you're thinking more along the lines of a plot for a novel, perhaps you've got a cast of a dozen, moving around between 20 locations (for a total of 32 characters plus places), starting out at about 24,000 words. Then let's throw in all 4 of the MICE elements, getting us to 96,000. And then divide all that by 1.5, and you've got 64,000 words, which is a pretty respectable starting point for a novel draft.

This equation isn't always precise, but it can often give you a rough idea of whether the idea you're looking at is a story or a novel. I often find the last step, dividing by 1.5, doesn't make sense for me personally. I write sparsely, but when I've done the math for things I've written, I find a lot of my pieces wind up closer to the "$L = (((C+P)*750)*M)$" portion of the equation. Sometimes, I'll carve a chunk of those words out when I edit, but I'm more likely to add words when I'm editing a piece, as I find things I've left out.

While the equation portion might be "your mileage may vary," the MICE Quotient can be a useful method of figuring out the story you want to tell and how to structure it. If the equation works for you as well, then awesome!

If not, don't worry about it. It's not perfect for everyone, and you don't have to do this math in order to write a novel. However, it can be an interesting way to estimate the length of something you're considering writing, and it may help you see how adding (or subtracting) characters, locations, and types of plots impact how long of a story or novel you wind up with.

~

Oh No, My Idea is Too Big

Sometimes, you've got a great idea with a bunch of moving parts and amazing characters and so many good subplots.

And then, after you've started writing, you realize your idea is too big. (If you're lucky, you might see the warning signs in advance, but that doesn't always happen.)

I've seen this happen in movies, where they try to cram in too many awesome things, which winds up making nothing really stand out. In a less jam-packed movie, you get great, memorable moments. In these crowded movies, you get more of a blur as they try to fit all the things into too little space.

How does this apply to writing advice? Well, sometimes, you have so many awesome ideas, you try to cram all of them into one story or novel. But by cramming in too much, you're forced to cut corners on all the awesome things, which then means they don't get enough room to be as cool as they could be. Sure, with a story or novel, you might not be bound by arbitrary limits on length in the same way a movie tends to be (though not always ... looking at you, *Lord of the Rings* expanded versions), but for most authors, there are common lengths of short stories and novels that are the goal. Going too much longer than the common lengths can make your piece a difficult sell, either to a market, an agent, or readers— not everyone has the bandwidth for "doorstopper" style books that quite literally could keep a heavy door from closing if placed in front of them. (I don't recommend books as ways to keep doors open, honestly. That's unkind to the books.)

So how do you remedy this? Unfortunately, the answer is often that you should limit the amount of awesome stuff you put in your story to give it the room it needs to breathe. Perhaps what you initially thought was one story turns out to be two separate stories (or novels). By splitting up a too big story, you can take each piece and let the neat elements of each one shine. Just like how sequels and spin-offs work in movies and TV, you could wind up with a duology or trilogy (or more), or you could find a way to divide your idea based on character arcs, for example, so one piece is a spin-off of the other. (And if you have an amazing, fan-favorite character, find a way to keep them in all the pieces. *cough* *Arya Stark* *cough*)

You may find that when the pieces are separated, one or the other is more appealing, and maybe that means one of the pieces doesn't get fully explored immediately. But you can save that piece for later and return to it when it seems appealing, or after you've finished the first one.

~

Too Many Ideas: Idea Tracking

If you're like me, you may often have more ideas than you know what to do with, and not enough time to implement them. But equally important is a method of tracking those ideas that works for you.

For a long time, I kept my ideas in a lot of places: I had a tag in my email, a section of the notes on my phone, and space in my writing spreadsheet (which serves a great many purposes). Some of them were snippets of dialogue or an interesting premise. With all these ideas collected, when I wanted something new to write, I could sift through the ideas to see if anything struck my fancy.

The downside was my ideas were scattered, so sometimes I had to hunt for the notes specific to a given idea. Sometimes, too, what I wrote down was insufficient to remember what I was thinking of at the time.

If you're new to writing, now is a perfect time to start thinking about how you want to track your ideas. It might be in a physical notebook, in a digital document (locally or in the cloud), or something else entirely. But it's worth thinking about how to collect the ideas you have into a location or form that will be most useful to you.

It's okay if you don't nail this on your first try, because your system isn't written in stone. (Unless, for some reason, you've decided the best way for you to track your ideas is to etch them into stone. However, I would suggest this might be the least portable version of an idea recording system, and you might want to rethink it from the start.) You can track your ideas in one way to begin with, and then if you figure out it's not working great for you, you can try something different.

If you've been writing for a while, you may already have a system that works. Or you might be looking for a system that works better for you, because you, like me, keep forgetting where you put that idea or what you were going to do with it when you got around to it. I have a couple of suggestions.

~

The Writer's Notebook

Writers love blank notebooks. We hoard blank notebooks sometimes, like we're dragons. We like to have a stack of blank notebooks waiting around for the right project.

For some authors, suggesting they use part of their precious hoard for writing notes is anathema. But I'm suggesting exactly that—picking one of the notebooks from your hoard and using it as a writer's notebook.

What do you put in a writer's notebook? A little bit of everything. It's a repository for ideas, but it can be so much more than that. You might write something experimental in such a notebook, and maybe you decide it's too weird for Present You, but Future You might look back on that experimental bit and see the shape of something they can work with.

Some writer's notebooks are messy places, while others are much more organized and tidier. You can use all sorts of organizational methods to keep track of what's in the notebook, or you can let chaos reign. You could do a combination of journal (or morning pages) and ideas and drafts and scraps. The possibilities are truly endless.

The idea of a writer's notebook isn't one I was familiar with initially. It's one of many methods writers find useful to collect their ideas. But in reading more about them, I realized my varying systems of keeping track of ideas could be a form of writer's notebook, mainly comprising digital forms of the concept. And some authors may prefer a digital notebook (which saves you the pain of using one of your hoarded notebooks).

But there's something satisfying about writing on paper now and then, even with all the technology at our fingertips. If you're a digital idea keeper, give a paper notebook a try to see if it changes the way you generate ideas or think about them, as an experiment.

~

DIY Idea Decks

The system I've moved to more recently is a do-it-yourself idea "deck." There are bunches of storytelling and writing decks available commercially (and I own quite a few of those, which I'll talk about). I took the basic concept of those decks and made my own.

For my DIY idea deck, I bought 3 by 5 index cards in 10 different colors. I then made a list of 10 different types of ideas I had strewn throughout my life (in the aforementioned notebooks, phone file, and emails). Finally, I tracked down where I'd stashed all my ideas and wrote each one on a card of an appropriate color.[3] If I had information about when I came up with the idea, I noted that as well. And in a few cases, when the ideas were things I got from another source or brainstormed with other writers, I jotted down who was involved in the genesis of the idea. (That way, if one of my ideas becomes something amazingly popular and lucrative, I will know who to thank when I get all the money and awards ... a girl can dream, right?)

Now, when I'm looking for an idea for something new to write, I can turn to my DIY idea deck. The largest chunk of my cards are the ones with a brief story seed or premise on them. These range from a few brief words to me squishing down my already small

---

[3] The colors don't mean anything; I assigned each color I had available to a category of idea. The only reason to make each one a different color is so I can look into my box of idea cards and say "ah, yes, I think I would like to look at potential titles today." Or whatever.

writing and filling every line of the index card with notes related to the idea. I can shuffle these index cards and draw a card at random, or I can flip through the cards until an idea jumps out at me.

Other categories I have for my DIY idea deck are names for characters, groups, locations, and more; titles I think would make an interesting story; quotes and song lyrics I want to base something on; and snippets of dialogue. This is a sample of the sorts of categories you might use if you're building something similar.

Once I've used an idea from my deck, I make a note at the bottom of the card (or on the back if I've run out of space on the front) about what story or poem I used the idea for and the date. I keep those cards, too, so I can look back at them and remember where I've used a given idea and when, in case I have a sudden recollection of an old idea but don't remember I've already used it.

If you like this system but don't want to use as much paper as I've used in making my DIY idea deck, there are programs and apps that let you construct something similar, but virtual. In many ways, that might be more useful, because then your ideas can live in the cloud, and you're not tied to shuffling through actual cards. You can also find programs and apps that let you do more of a "thought mapping" process, which can be a great way to collect multiple ideas as you work on putting together a novel, or a place to record and jump from one idea to another as they occur to you.

~

All Out of Ideas? Try Commercial Idea Decks

I've accumulated a large collection of card-based writing tools, each of which is useful to different parts of my writing process. Some of them are great for character development, some are wonderful for putting together a plot, and some are designed to help you write yourself out of a dead end or corner. (If you're curious about my favorites, check out the Appendix for a short summary of the decks I have and what I use them for.)

Much of my collection is card-based, but there are also some that include dice. You can find a ton of writer's dice sets at online retailers (and possibly at some physical retailers). These sets tend to be more focused on a specific genre, so there might be one for mystery writers or kids who want to write. If you're only interested in a single genre, they can be particularly useful, but if you write across genres, you could wind up with a whole lot of dice in order to have the right set for whatever you're working on.

Most of the card-based tools I have are designed to work in more than one genre, though some of them have some genre-specific expansions or aspects. In many cases, there are ways to include or exclude specific genres as needed. In other cases, it requires more mental gymnastics to figure out how to take a fantasy-oriented idea and recast it for something appropriate to a sci-fi setting, or vice versa.

Possibly the most important thing to know about any sort of writing tool of this nature is they can be both tools and distractions. You can have a lot of fun looking at the cards and plotting out all sorts of interesting ideas. But in the end, you still have to write those ideas. So it's important to not get too distracted by the fun of the cards and remember they're a tool in your arsenal to make writing happen.

~

To Outline or Not To Outline

I was a pantser[4] once.

Until I took an arrow to the knee.

No, that's not quite true. But I was a pantser when I first started writing. I let the story take me where it wanted to.

And thus, in my first NaNoWriMo, I reached 50,000 words, and my story was a mess. My protagonist team had arrived at the place where they were supposed to learn all about who they were. This should have happened in the first third of the book, based on

---

[4] "Pantser" refers to people who "write by the seat of their pants," or without an outline. The opposite is "plotter," the people who outline everything before they can start writing. There are also hybrids, like "plantsers" (or "planters"), which involves starting without an outline but developing something resembling a plan as you go. People in each of these categories have successfully written novels, so they're all valid, as long as they work for you.

my Grand Vision, which was not an outline. It was "just vibes," as the kids say these days.

This recurred on other projects I worked on. I'd forget about something I really wanted to include. The plot would meander until it hit a wall. Or the brilliant idea I had would slip away before I had a chance to do anything with it.

I started outlining my subsequent novels. But then I realized my short stories could also benefit from outlines, and I started writing those up as well.

Outlining novels is different from outlining short stories. In novels, you're looking at multiple arcs, all sorts of attempts and failures, and so much more. For most short stories, you're looking at a single arc and maybe a couple of try-fail-try again cycles, depending on the length of the story. But the basic principle remains the same.

When I outline my short stories, the outline usually answers a few questions:

1.   How and where does the story start? What thing has happened that makes this story worth telling?
2.   How does the protagonist try to fix it?
3.   How does that go wrong?
4.   How do they try to fix that?
5.   How does it resolve?

Sounds super simple, right?

You can use this same format for outlining a novel, though you will probably add a few reiterations of questions 3 and 4.

If this format is simpler than you want, you can find a load of books about outlining novels in different genres. My personal favorite is Mark Teppo's *Jumpstart Your Novel*, though sometimes I get a little frustrated by the structure presented in the book and fall back on an older version of his structure I outlined a handful of my earlier novel attempts with. Many authors also recommend the *Save the Cat* series, which was originally for screenwriting, but which has added a version for novels to help with the story structure depending on what kind of story you want to tell.

There are also tons of outlining methods you can find online. So if outlining your novel is something you want to do, you can poke around at different methods to see which one works best for you.

If you don't want to outline your novel, and simply let it take you where it wants to, instead, that's a valid way to write as well. There's a reason we have the terms pantser and plotter (and plantser or planter) in the writing world. And there are many authors who can pants their way through a novel or a series. I think those people have a rough outline they're able to hold in their head as they go. I can't do that. I need to have my outline in a place where I can refer to it, and my brain is unreliable.

As you work through the process of writing a novel, you may find a preference for pantsing or plotting. It can be an interesting exercise to try both methods to find which one works best for you. And there's nothing saying you can't choose the other for a specific project that needs to be more free-flowing or more concrete.

~

Time

I had a chat with a friend of mine several years back, where he mentioned wanting to write but never having time for it. He asked how I got so much done with a full-time job, running a craft business and a magazine (at the time), and having hobbies (like gaming, which is how the two of us know each other).

I told him my main trick was writing during my lunch break. I'd finished the first draft of a novel in about nine weeks by doing so. I also write three nights a week and at least part of the day on Saturdays and Sundays.

In this friend's case, his lunch break was when he socializes with co-workers and reads the news. He also has a million other things going on evenings and weekends. For him, like a lot of people, giving up that much free time is something they're unwilling or unable to do. But I've decided I'd rather spend my free time writing. It means I'm behind on dozens of TV shows and haven't seen many new, popular movies. For me, that's an acceptable trade off reflecting my own priorities. And there's nothing wrong with having different priorities.

The trick, however, is if you want to write, you have to make time for it, one way or another. For some people, it means getting up early or staying up late. For others, it means squeezing in fifteen minutes (or more) wherever you can find it. Your schedule may mean you don't have one consistent time of day when you can squeeze in some writing, so you have to write at varying times during any given day.

But even if you only manage a single typed page a day (roughly 250 words, or so my documents tell me), you could have 365 pages in a year, or around 91,250 words. And that's way longer than my books tend to run in draft format (or in finished format). Even 100 words a day or a single page each week adds up, especially if you're writing short stories instead of novels. But you can also plug away at a novel in small chunks, extending the writing over years if necessary.

It ends up being about making writing a priority for you, and then keeping it in that position, especially when you could be doing other things that are less work. It's not easy to do in a work-centric culture that expects everything you do to be in service of the almighty dollar (or currency of your location). But even if you're only writing for yourself, it can be a valid hobby, side gig, or whatever you like to call it.

~

When Is the Best Time to Write?

There's a lot of writing advice telling new authors they should write every day, they should make time in their schedule for writing, and so on. And while in an ideal world, authors could write every day, the reality of life is many of us don't have that luxury. Instead, I would suggest what's more valuable for new authors is learning when the best time for them to write is and attempting to make good use of that knowledge.

I get up on the early side, even when I work from home. But I also know I'm not at my best in the morning. I can read emails and social media, maybe play some games, but I won't be able to write coherent words. I work "standard" hours, and while I'm working, I'm only able to make quick notes if a story idea comes to me.

However, I'm fastidious about taking an hour-long lunch as frequently as I'm able to, which winds up being most days. During my lunch break, I can get some writing tasks done—I can usually work on blog posts or updating my records of story rejections (and acceptances). Sometimes, I can send stories out on submission. But I can also write during that hour—if I'm working on a novel, it's not unusual for me to write about 1,000 words or one scene during my lunch break, even with time to prepare and eat my food. If I'm doing a monthly challenge, my lunch break is also typically adequate to write a poem or maybe a rough draft of a flash fiction piece, too.

The bulk of my writing time, however, comes in the evenings, after work. Then I've got a chunk of time sometimes as long as three hours, if we have a quick dinner or I start working on things while I'm eating. That gives me time to work on short stories, other blog posts, story submissions, and any other writing tasks. So arguably, that would be my most productive writing time.

The real secret for me, though, is if I can struggle through the first hour or so of not being fully awake in the morning on the weekends, I can get a lot more writing done if I start my day with it. So ideally, I should structure my mornings differently during the week, too, so perhaps I could get some good writing in before I start my day job.

That's hard for me, though. Getting up early in the morning is not something that comes naturally to me. An earlier bedtime might help, but it might also allow me to get more sleep than usual. So I have to balance my desire to sleep and my desire to get writing time. And honestly, the former often wins out.

But other authors might be perfectly suited to burning the late-night hours, and they may have their most productive writing time then. And others might be able to work with fifteen minutes here and there where they can grab the time. The trick is to look at your day and your writing tasks and figure out what you can make work for you. Maybe that's the same time, every day, for an hour at a time. Maybe it's the moments you can steal on the bus or on a break from work. But knowing what works best for you is a matter of trial and error. Ultimately, it's about writing when you can and not worrying about arbitrary goals of writing daily or producing a set number of words every day. One sentence a day is one more sentence than you had previously, and that's progress!

~

Figuring Out Your Pace

I wasn't good at setting and hitting deadlines until I had a sense of how long it takes me to write and revise pieces of different lengths. Figuring out your pace makes it easier to plan different projects and determine whether you can meet a self-imposed or external deadline. And while outliers can and do happen, they become much rarer when you understand your writing pace (and revising pace, but that's a different section).

Because I've been writing for a while now, I'm generally able to look at a story idea and have a rough sense of how long of a story it's going to be (sometimes using the equation I talked about in the section on ideas). This isn't always foolproof. Sometimes I get partway into writing what I think is going to be a short story and realize it's actually a novella or longer. But by and large, if I set out to write a short story, I know roughly how long it will be and, more importantly in this case, about how long it will take me to write it.

One of the ways to learn your pace as a writer is to set a timer for a given amount of time and start writing. I recommend doing this several times, potentially on different projects or different types of writing. For example, if you're writing a primarily dialogue scene, and you have a good sense of your characters, you might be able to write more words in a set period of time than you would be able to if you're writing an action scene. Or you may be the opposite. But the trick is to do a few of these "sprints" and then calculate your average words per minute or hour.[5]

---

[5] This can also be used to figure out when the best time to write is for you, by seeing how many words you write in comparable sprints at

While that pace may change occasionally, and while you may become a faster writer as you get more practice, it's a good starting point to help you figure out how long it will take you to write a project.

During NaNoWriMo, for example, I'm attempting to write 50,000 words over 30 days. By the NaNoWriMo system, that means writing approximately 1,667 words a day. If I know I can write 500 words in half an hour, I'd need to set aside about an hour and forty-five minutes to get through my word count for the day. I might give myself two hours, to make sure I can hit my goal, and maybe exceed it a little, which will make the rest of the month a bit easier for me. (That also allows me to take a day off now and then, which almost always happens during November for one reason or another.)

If, instead, I'm writing a short story that I expect to be about 3,000 words when it's done, I can theoretically write that story in three hours. That seems fast to a lot of authors, but this is after years of practice. (And in reality, I'll probably work on the story in half-hour blocks over a few weeks, because I'm also working on other things at the same time, and if I sit down and write a short story in one sitting of three hours, I won't be able to make any more words for the rest of the day—written or verbal.)

Knowing my pace means if I have a deadline for a piece, I can work backward from the deadline to figure out when I need to start it by, in order to finish on time. But it isn't only the writing time I need to calculate (yeah, I know, more math, but it's easier math this time), because writing a piece involves three factors: writing, letting it sit, and revising. I usually look at these in terms of weeks—it'll likely take me X weeks to write a piece and Y weeks to revise it. I want to let it sit for at least one week in between writing and revising, so my equation is $X + Y + 1$. If the number of weeks the equation gives me is equal to or less than the number of weeks before the deadline, I can do it without much difficulty. It's when the result of the equation is greater than the number of weeks before the deadline that I need to start panicking. (Or, as some have said, letting the deadline make a whooshing sound as it passes

different times of day.

by—also known as not taking on the project and deadline in question.)

So if you're an author who has difficulty meeting deadlines, the first thing you should do is make an honest assessment of your pace for writing a story (or novel, or whatever the deadline involves). Without knowing your pace in the first place, you're likely to run into missed deadlines and overcommitting yourself. But once you've got your pace in mind, you can evaluate if a proposed deadline is possible. And then, assuming it is, you can set out to hit it.

~

The Amazing Tomato Timer

No, it's not actually called the Amazing Tomato Timer, though those do exist.

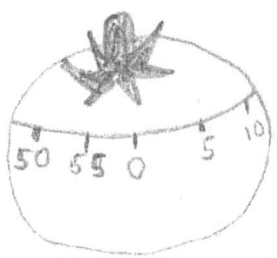

What it's really called is the Pomodoro Method. Pomodoro, however, means "tomato" in Italian, so some authors reference tomatoes when they're talking about the Pomodoro Method.

The method itself is simple. Set a timer for twenty minutes. While the time is ticking down, write. When the timer goes off, take a break for ten or twenty minutes. Then repeat.

The Pomodoro Method can be a good starting point if you want to get some data on how quickly you write. It can also be a great way to get some focused writing time. For me, knowing I only need to work on the thing I'm working on for twenty minutes makes it easier for me to get started on it.

Sometimes, I get to the end of my sprint and keep going. Other times, I section out my time in twenty-minute increments, followed by ten-minute breaks when I do something different.

And some days, the distractions are everywhere, and this method doesn't work well for me. But I find it works more often than it doesn't, so it's a great trick to have in my arsenal.

~

Trying to Make the Novel Go Zoom

So you've figured out your brilliant ideas, and you've carved out time when you can write. Awesome!

I said in the previous section that all you really need to write a novel is ideas and time. That might not be ALL you need. Because you also have to write it. And that, in and of itself, is not easy. So this is the part of the book where I share my thoughts on trying to zoom through the writing and the stumbling blocks you may encounter along the way.

~

Parts of a Novel

Beginnings are Hard

Time and again, I return to the same problem: starting something new is hard.

I often have story or novel ideas where I know exactly what needs to happen. But I don't always know how the story starts or where it starts. I can easily get 1,500 words into a new idea before I realize the plot hasn't started yet. I might be having fun writing a character and their interactions with their environment or other characters, but the story isn't getting anywhere. And then I have a hard time getting the character to where something interesting could happen.

Even when I know exactly what the interesting thing is, it doesn't always seem right to throw the character straight into it, either. So that means it's time for me to reconsider what the plot is and where it needs to start to make it work.

Other times, I know what the beginning should be—exactly how to kick things off—but I need to look at the larger picture of the whole story before I can make that opening work. This generally means my idea is cool, but it needs a little bit more work to see where that fits into the story I want to tell.

Beginnings are always hard, but sometimes you have to try things out to see what sticks. When you're writing a novel, you may find you need to do a bit of metaphorical "throat clearing" before your novel can get going. You may wind up writing chapters that, when you get to the end, you can identify as that throat-clearing exercise, and you may also realize you should cut those from the novel in order to start with a stronger beginning.

It might seem like you wasted time with those chapters, and you may resist removing them. In the end, those chapters are useful to the writing process, as they allowed you to work your way into the plot, and they probably told you important things about your characters and/or setting. They are, in a way, a bit of prewriting.

And you can always save them for bonus content for your readers once the novel's been published. But that's much, much farther in the future.

~

Where Do I Start?

A friend of mine once asked if I always start writing at the same place. They wanted to know if I started with a scene, character, descriptions, or dialogue, as well as whether I wrote my scenes in order, wrote them in reverse order, or, in their words, "Write the punchline and then construct the elaborate justification for it?"

My stories and novels generally start with an idea seed. "Wouldn't it be cool if ...?" Sometimes that comes in the format of a scene or a snippet of dialogue, but more often, it's not much more than an idea. And sometimes, once I start prodding at the idea, it falls apart, like a rotten seed. So then I sweep up the bits and file them away, in case they somehow grow back together in a different configuration.

Once I have more than the idea seed, the next thing I personally must have is character names. I can have ideas for the characters, but until they have names, they don't become real enough to me to consider writing. Once I've got the names set for a story, it's odd for me to change them, too. I think there's something about naming the character that locks them into my mind, and once they've got a name, changing it feels weird. (Also, there was the time I changed a character's name from Lance to Athos and wasn't careful with my find and replace. That was the time I learned how frequently I use the word "glanced". Hello, "gAthosd".)

Once I've got something larger than an idea seed and names, I generally put together a rough outline for the story, and then I write it, start to finish. I have heard about people who write their stories backwards (whether that's the final scene or the final line), but that method doesn't work for me. There are occasions when I finish a story and realize it needs a different beginning, but that's about the closest I would come to writing backwards. For me, there are more often occasions where I write a few scenes at the beginning I then realize won't be necessary (that "throat clearing" I mentioned before), and they get cut from the story later. But even if I have a solid outline that could permit me to jump around and write different scenes, I prefer to write them start to finish.

I'm the same way with novels, too. I have to write them from start to finish, without jumping around. If I'm working on a novel and realize something I've already written needs to be altered in order to work with something I write later, I make a note to myself about the change and continue forward. For me, going back and reworking those earlier parts makes me lose momentum.

Of course, not everyone is like that. I have a friend who prefers to write scenes completely out of order, based on what scene she wants to write when she sits down to her manuscript, and it works for her. If I did this, I would write all the "fun" scenes and then struggle with every other scene I still needed to write. It would mean I'd never write those scenes with combat in them because I hate them.

Other authors will leave notes to themselves when they get to a scene that needs more research or they don't want to write yet. I try to do as much of my research in advance to avoid that part of the problem. But if I suddenly realize I need to know a detail to go forward, I will pause my writing and do the research. If it's a minor detail, I'll flag it with a comment to check it later. And I will usually try to check that as soon as I'm done writing that chunk of the piece, so the comment doesn't hang out for too long.

So for me, it's everything in order, because getting through those less fun scenes means they exist when I am "done" with writing the novel ... or at least the first draft.

~

Combat Scenes and Other Things You Hate to Write

AKA: Why can't we all just get along?
I admit it. I hate writing combat scenes. Dread them, even. I don't like reading them, either. My mind sort of glazes over, waiting to get back to the "good stuff," also known as the part where they aren't fighting any more. But I write action and adventure and superheroes, and these genres include combat scenes. So I've had to buckle down and write them, whether I want to or not.

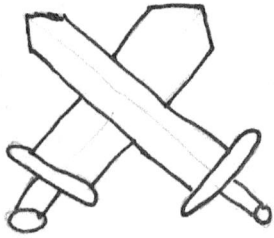

I'm still not sure I'm good at writing combat scenes. I tend to try to keep them short—no long, drawn-out battles for me. And since most of my characters are working from a moral center that says killing is wrong, they tend to be combats that simply subdue the opposing force. But that can be tricky in and of itself, since you want to have the characters use enough force to stop the bad guys, but not too much force. So it's a balancing act.

The trick I generally use when I absolutely must include a combat scene in what I'm writing involves starting with a simple version of the scene in which I block out the details and don't worry about writing good sentences. You could think of it like stage directions and write things like "Character A swings a sword at Character B, but Character B doesn't get hit. Then Character B stabs Character A." Then, once you've got that framework in place, you can fill in details and have all the grimaces and grunts and groans you need.

Maybe you don't mind writing combat scenes, but there are other scenes you don't enjoy writing. This same sort of simple version of the scene that you then flesh out can work for that.

But sometimes, the reason you hate writing a scene is because you find it boring to write. And if you think it's boring to write, the odds are high your readers might find it boring to read.

If that's the case, you might ask yourself, "do I really need this scene?" But the better question to ask is "what does this scene accomplish?" Sometimes, the "boring" scene isn't accomplishing anything, and it's a pause on the way between cool plot thing A and cool plot thing B. That might mean you could not write the scene at all.

But the other way to fix a "boring" scene is to give it a purpose. Even if it is a pause between exciting scenes, it doesn't mean it can't be used to accomplish something. Maybe your characters need to have a long conversation, and you're dreading writing so much dialogue. But maybe if that dialogue takes place while your characters are running for their lives from a dragon, robot army, horde of zombies, or whatever fits your genre, the scene will suddenly be a lot more interesting for you to write.

All that being said, I've been told a lot of conversation in a combat scene isn't realistic, so maybe "on the run" isn't a great time for a deep conversation either. But there are ways you can revitalize what would otherwise be a "boring" scene to write by starting with sketches rather than full-blown paintings, or by mixing up the scene by adding an interesting element to it that makes it more fun to write.

~

Stuck in the Middle with You

Sometimes, my stories and novels grind to a halt around the middle. Pinpointing the reason for this isn't always easy, but for me, at least, it's often because I don't know what happens at the end, or I'm not sure how the story is going to go from Point B (the middle) to Point C (the end). Sometimes, getting stuck in the middle means I should look at my outline more closely and see where it's falling apart.

Because my novels absolutely must have outlines, the other issue I run into when I get stuck in this bog of the middle is that the first half or so of my outline is clear about what happens. Around that middle part, though, things get vague. Maybe I included something like "something happens to make the main character realize something" (in exactly those words). That means I need to do some additional ore plotting to figure out what that event and realization actually are. Sometimes the answer is further on in the novel, and sometimes it's not. (Just because I write outlines for everything doesn't necessarily mean Past Me included all the needed details in the outline.)

However, there's also the concept of the "murky middle." When you've been working on a project for a while, you may get so bogged down in what you've been doing that you think you'll never get it done. Sometimes, this can be solved if you can give yourself a break from the writing and do something else. However, if you're working under a deadline (self-imposed or otherwise), taking that break might seem impossible.

I'll talk more about breaks later, but the quick version here is: sometimes, a short break is exactly what you need, allowing you to return to the project refreshed, and thus getting yourself out of the murky middle.

Other times, the only solution is to power through it with the knowledge that once you get past that point, you'll pick up steam again. It can be valuable to think of writing a novel as like climbing a hill so you can sled down it. Going uphill, dragging your sled through the snow, is always slow going. But when you get to the top and get on the sled, you zip to the bottom of the hill. The second half of many novels goes much faster than the first half does, because you're sledding downhill to that conclusion.

If you're not someone who outlines, and you find yourself stuck in the middle of your novel, you may need to figure out the end. Or, if you already know the end, you may have to take the time to figure out how you get from where you are to where you should be. In this way, outlines (no matter how sketchy) can be a lot like road maps, which keep you on the road rather than getting stuck offroad in mud halfway up your wheel wells. (Some people do that for fun and call it "mudding". I have never understood those people.)

~

Falling Off the Map

A similar, and yet different, problem with the middle of a novel can be when your story takes on a life of its own and somehow falls off the edge of your map.

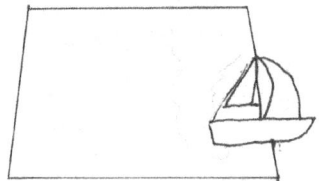

Many folks who fall into the "pantsers" camp of writing insist they let their characters show them where they should go. As a member of the "plotter" camp, I have to be more careful about that. Because my characters are jerks—fascinating jerks, but still jerks. If I let them do whatever they like, they're likely to wander around, avoid the plot, and otherwise lay waste to my carefully laid plans. And when they do that, more often than not, I write myself into a corner and then have to figure out how to get out of that corner.

How to avoid wandering characters? Sometimes, the answer is to let them wander some, with the full knowledge that what you're writing is probably going to be cut. If you're trying to make more efficient use of your time, however, that can be an issue. In that case, it helps to check in with your outline (if you have one) occasionally to make sure your characters haven't gone off in some unplanned direction. If you don't have an outline, this is another place where you should pause to think about where your characters have led you, and how to get them back to the plot you want to write.

(As a note, sometimes when your characters wander off, that can be a sign that they know where they're going, and maybe your outline or vague plan isn't what the story needs to be. So there's value in taking a step back and considering whether this new direction is preferable to the old one, or whether you're going to have to pull those characters off the brink and back onto your map.)

~

And Then There's the End

Figuring out where to end a story or novel can be tricky. I like to have my endings all tied up neatly, and I like to end things with someone saying or doing something clever. To me, that's the most satisfying kind of ending—all is well in the world, and someone gets a clever quip that sticks with you. What's better is when that "final word" can encapsulate the entire story you've set out to tell. It can be difficult to get it right, but when it works, it's perfection.

For some pieces, I can see my way to the end when I get started. I know where the goalpost is, and I have to proceed toward it (even if it's not always in a straight line). For other pieces, it's much harder for me to pin down the ending. This is often when I have a vague idea of "these things should happen, and then ???" For me, figuring out the ending starts at the beginning, so I can set out a road map of what needs to happen to get there.

What this tells me is I should nail down those endings before I get started. And while that seems counterintuitive to people who are discovery writers or pantsers, it makes it easier for me to write the story if I know where it's going. I enjoy finding a twist I didn't see coming as I'm writing, but when I know the ending, I can evaluate if that twist will work or require a change to my ending. And nine times out of ten, I don't want to change my ending. That remaining one time out of ten is when I decide the twist will give me a new, better, ending.

On the flip side, I've written things where a beta reader read my story and then emailed me to make sure they had gotten the whole file. "That's it? That's how it ends?" they would ask. And in general, the answer was yes. That may mean I'm not the most qualified person to talk about how to write endings.

Ultimately, the most important thing to remember is you want the ending to be satisfying to your readers. You as the author should like it too, but if your readers don't like it, it could spoil an otherwise great story. So those beta readers not being sure about my ending is a good sign I should wrap things up differently, possibly by adding a bit more denouement (I do tend to rush my endings) or a beat or two more to let things settle and sink in. Then, my zinger of an ending can really shine!

~

The REALLY Hard Parts

It's always an adventure to start in on a new novel, even when I've got my outline firmly in hand. But though my rational brain tells me whatever I put on paper first doesn't have to be a super clever opening line, my emotional brain tells me I should start out with something so utterly amazing it will, of course, be the first line of the book.

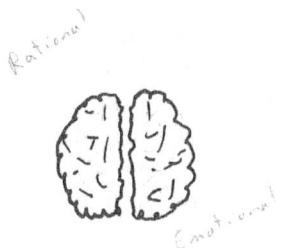

Sorry, emotional brain. Rational brain wins out in this situation, or else this book is never going to be written.

First drafts don't have to be perfect, and neither do first pages or first lines of those first drafts. Getting words on paper is key when you're first starting a new project. Editing is when the magic will happen, but you can't edit until you've got words to begin with.

So kick it off with a bang of some sort, even if it's not quite as perfect as you want, and tidy it up later. Throw the characters into some steaming mess and then get them out of it and on to the next mess. (It's messes all the way down.)

~

Identifying and Fixing a Flawed Story

As I've written more and more, I've reached a point now where I can draft a story and often see that it's a flawed story. Sometimes, I've grabbed onto something too big for the scope of a short story. Other times, not much is happening in what I've written. To be clear, this isn't a flaw in the writing, but rather a flaw with the plot I'm trying to use.

When it comes to novels, you might not see this sort of plot flaw until you've gotten quite a few words down, which can be disheartening. You might get to the end before you realize the flaws.

If you reach this point with your novel, whether during the drafting or after you've finished the first draft, don't despair. While you may have a lot of work ahead of you, you've also got a bunch of material to work with. If you decide to set the project aside, the experience of having written it will help inform your future writing and plotting.

Reaching a point where you can identify plot flaws in your own writing is a valuable skill to learn. It does take time to hone, and in the meantime, you may write a lot of stuff that feels unsalvageable, once you realize the flaw is baked into the entire piece.

The corollary to this skill is figuring out how to fix a flawed story or novel. And sometimes, you might not be at the stage of your writing career where you have that skill. I'm still working on it, personally. Even if I can locate the various flaws, it doesn't mean I can come up with the solution to repair those flaws. Sometimes, a flawed story is not able to be fixed. But other times, the story can be fixed, but maybe not at the present time.

When I come across one of my stories I've identified as flawed, but I'm not sure how to fix it, there are two choices in my mind. The first is to completely rewrite the story with a new approach and likely a new plot. Sometimes the characters need a few tweaks too. Starting over from scratch sucks, but sometimes the fresh perspective is good. And there's nothing saying you can't borrow some parts of your first draft as you re-draft the piece.

The second alternative is to file the story away and come back to it later. I know I'm always learning new techniques and tricks in my writing, even after spending more than a decade working on my craft. Sometimes, today's problem can't be solved with today's knowledge, but it can be solved with tomorrow's knowledge. So every once in a while, when I'm looking for a project to work on and don't have any new ideas, I sift through my partial stories folder and see what gems I've got hiding in there. Sometimes, learning something new over the course of writing more stories shows me the way to fix that flawed story months or years after I had to set it aside. And it's always a nice feeling to be able to pull something from the partial stories folder, fix it up, and send it out into the world to find a home. It's magnificent when those stories find their homes, because I was willing to give them and myself time to figure out how to fix them.

It's a good idea, if you're going to set a story aside, to make sure you've made some notes about where you planned to go with it. Even if those notes are things along the lines of "I'm not sure how to get my main characters from here to the ending," as long as you also note what the ending you're thinking of is. Don't be like me and open an old file to find a made-up German-sounding word with no details about what it was intended for. You'll yell at your past self at that point. (But that story wound up working out and getting published, so maybe the made-up German-sounding word meant "you can do it!")

Sometimes, backburnering the project is the better choice. This doesn't mean you'll never come back to it, but it's not the book you're able to write at the current moment, which is likely why it feels like a huge slog to get through the needed work every day.

It can be a difficult decision to give up, even temporarily, on a project you've been working on. After all, there's plenty of advice in the writing world saying finishing things is important. And while this is ultimately true, it also does a disservice to authors who take it to mean "you must finish the thing you have started before you start another thing." It's perfectly fine to put a project on the backburner and come back to it later. The trick is making yourself actually come back to it later.

If your project is already outlined, it's easier to set it aside and pick it up again later. You may have forgotten some of the details of what you had planned, but with a robust enough outline, you can generally reread what you've written, reread the outline, and be ready to write on the project again.

If you haven't outlined your project and choose to stop, it can be worth taking a bit of time to jot down some notes (potentially in the file where you've been writing the novel, so they're easy to find later) about where you were going and what the reasons for stopping are, so you'll have a bit of a guide when you come back to the project.

If you find yourself stuck while writing your novel, ask yourself if it's something you might want to backburner until you're ready to write it. While that's not always an option, sometimes it is, and sometimes it can give you the break you need so when you do write it, it's done well.

And one last thing. If you reach a point where your novel plot (or a story plot) feels like it's a huge disaster, and it will never see the light of day, DO NOT delete the file. Put it away, if you like, but keep it. Someday, you might find you're ready to tackle it again, using the knowledge you've gained in the intervening time.

If At First You Don't Succeed

It's important to remember that while the goal of writing a novel is to finish and publish it, the process doesn't look the same for every author. It's also completely reasonable to write a novel for yourself. Maybe no one else will ever read it, or maybe you'll share it with a few close friends or family members.

It's not necessary to suffer through writing a novel, either. Yes, it is work, but if it isn't making you happy to write it, it's worth asking yourself if there are ways you can change things to make yourself happy, or if putting it aside (temporarily or for good) would be better.

While this may seem like counterintuitive advice for a book about writing a novel, I think it's important to write what makes you happy. And if that means writing something that isn't a novel, do it! Even though it's hard for someone who wants to be a novelist to give up on that dream, you can still be a writer simply by virtue of writing.

It's hard for writers to abandon something they've put a lot of work into, but sometimes, it's the best solution for something that isn't working. You may still find pieces of the first version you can work into the new version, or you may find the first version is a prewriting exercise that will make the new version better.

~

Writing Complications

When I say writing complications, I'm not talking about how to write more and more problems for your characters to deal with. I'm talking about the complications in a writer's life that cause difficulties in being able to write. There are a lot of factors involved here, but for this section, I'm mainly talking about the ones that cut into your time—things like day jobs and travel.

~

Writing When You Work from Home

When I'm working my day job in the office, I'm able to draw a solid line between work and writing. I can get a little bit of writing stuff done in the morning before my workday starts and during my lunch break. When the pandemic began and we switched to work from home, it became harder to use those same pieces of time for writing. In the mornings, I would stay in bed a little longer (a benefit of no commute), and during my lunch break, I would often do chores around the apartment—all those things that always needed doing but were never convenient to do when I worked in an office five days a week.

Then when the day ended, I didn't have my commute home, but it meant I had some more time for chores and cooking from scratch, which meant making dinner took a little more time. I could then sit back down at my computer after dinner and write, but there wasn't the necessary division between staring at the work laptop screen and staring at the personal laptop screen.

In those early days of the pandemic, I found I could get more writing done if I could get away from my computer for a bit. I printed out a copy of what I needed to work on and sat in a different part of the apartment. This let me still work on a writing task while not being in front of my computer.

Soon, though, I decided to clear off an old desk that had been a landing area for stuff after the desktop computer that used to sit on it had died. Having that space cleaned up for my work computer meant I could have a "commute"—however many steps it took me to cross the living room and into the dining room. It might not be much, but physically moving from one to the other (rather than always being in the same seat) helped reestablish that separation between work and writing.

I was fortunate to have the option to have two different workspaces in my apartment. Not everyone has that luxury. But if you have the ability, it can be super useful to establish the place you work on day job things and the place you work on writing things. If you only have a single computer and space, try things like setting up two different screen modes or color shifts on your computer, so the screen looks different when you're working as opposed to when you're writing. You can automate this under some operating systems, so your computer can automatically shift the screen mode or color at the end of your workday. Having a little change can help your brain accept that it's now time for it to work on something different.

~

Writing with A Hybrid Work Schedule

After two and a half years of working from home (with occasional days when I was the only person in the office, to water plants, check the mail, and make sure everything was still running as it should be), my job implemented a hybrid work policy. The policy took into consideration people's position and needs, but because my position was considered one of the essential ones, it meant I was expected to work from the office three days a week, if my workload and schedule permitted.

Unfortunately, because of other things on my schedule, I worked from the office on the days when I typically got the most writing done during the week. But with my normal commute added back into the mix, I "finished" my day almost an hour after I finished when I was working from home, which cut down on the amount of time I had to work on writing. In addition, working in the office and commuting often took a larger toll on my energy levels than rolling out of bed half an hour before I started work and moving to the other side of the room at the end of the day. So I found I needed to rebalance my expectations of what was possible to do on a weeknight on the days I worked in the office.

This also meant my weekend writing time became more valuable to me, as I could often get a larger chunk of time to write, and I could often do several of these chunks with short breaks in between. This meant I had to reconfigure my writing schedule, so I was only working on one or two tasks on weeknights and saving other tasks for weekends. I also experimented with doing more "business" of writing tasks (blog posts, social media, story submissions) on weeknights and writing and revising pieces on weekends.

After a couple of months of experimentation, I'd come to some conclusions. Working in the office, along with the commute, was EXHAUSTING. Not only did I have to wake up earlier to catch my bus downtown, but I also did a lot more physical activity on days I was in the office (the office space is much larger than our apartment, plus the restroom is at the opposite end of the floor from our space). The added physical activity was a good thing, but it wore me out. Getting home later was also a rough adjustment, because it meant immediately scrambling to get dinner ready and less cooking from scratch.

I was able to adjust back to getting things done on my lunch break, but it was almost all "business" stuff, almost never creative work. And while it was good to get that out of the way, with being exhausted when I got home, creative work sometimes had to take a back burner to doing something a bit more relaxing or mindless.

As more companies and jobs implement hybrid work policies (or fully end remote work), you may find you lose some momentum for your writing, if you were able to write at all during the pandemic (I know a lot of authors who could not). It can be incredibly useful to track your time and energy levels at different points in the day to help you figure out how to best optimize the time you spend writing and working on "business" tasks.

But it's also important to be gentle with yourself and not get frustrated if your output suddenly decreases. Capitalism is harsh, and it puts a crimp in creative pursuits of all kinds. So try not to despair, and work on what you can, when you can. Even incremental progress is progress!

~

Writing While Traveling

Sometimes, the thing getting in the way of writing isn't work but leisure. If you're traveling, your schedule tends to be upended, as does your "home" environment, whether a hotel or staying with friends or family. Or heck, even camping! So how do you get writing work done when you're outside of your normal schedule and residence?

Well, first off, maybe you don't. Maybe you take time to recharge and not get any writing done. However, if you're operating under deadlines, sometimes you need to do at least some writing work while you're traveling.

For me, a lot of my travel involves airplanes. It's not always convenient to use a laptop on a plane (especially when you wind up in the middle seat) or when you're waiting at the gate for your flight, so I like to have a notebook and pen if I hope to write during plane travel. Writing longhand is MUCH slower for me—I hold my writing implements in a convoluted way, and it makes my hand cramp up if I write too much. But it works, albeit at a slower pace. Pen and paper can also be useful if you're going somewhere where you won't have electricity or Wi-Fi. An alternative is sometimes putting notes into a phone using whatever note-taking app you have, though again, it can be slow going, between the tiny keyboard and autocorrect.

When we travel, our destination is typically somewhere with electricity and Wi-Fi, in which case we often bring our laptops, because we almost always have some downtime when our schedule isn't filled. When we go to the East Coast, for example, we're often able to stay up until what seems like midnight to folks there, but it's only 9 p.m. on the West Coast. And when they don't want to get moving until about noon their time, that's 9 a.m. for us.

Maintaining our West Coast schedule means there are a few hours in the morning to get some things done, even if we've got a full day of sightseeing planned. This doesn't work for everyone, of course, and can be anti-productive when East Coast folks visit the West Coast, and time is all jumbled up.

When we're traveling within our own time zone, there always tend to be a few hours here and there where we can steal a bit of time to work on something. And while it may not necessarily be a productive time for writing something new, sometimes that time can work for editing or other "business" of writing sorts of things not involving new words.

If there's something I absolutely 100 percent need to write new words on, though, that necessitates carving out a bit of time in the schedule and holing up with my laptop. It can be hard for social and mental reasons. Getting into a writing headspace when you're not in the right physical space can be rough. Hotel desks and chairs never feel quite the same as my dining room table and folding chair. And if we're staying with friends or family, the only place to sit and write can frequently be the bed. So I might try to find a coffee shop, which might not quite be the place I'm used to, but at least it has the coffee shop ambiance I've experienced before. It's about tricking your brain to believe things are as close to normal as you can make them, sometimes.

While others may find different tricks to help them get writing done while they're traveling, having alternatives, sneaking in writing when I can, and trying to recreate my home (or coffee shop) writing experience can all be helpful if I need to get writing things done while traveling. And sometimes, I give myself a break from writing while I'm on vacation!

~

When Your Day Job is Writing Too

Some fiction authors find themselves drawn to day jobs that also take advantage of their writing skills. But if you have a day job involving a lot of writing, you can end up in a position where both your day job and your hobby (or secondary job) involve putting words on paper, which can wind up limiting your creativity in one or both venues.

The flip side of this, however, is the more writing you do, the more your writing can improve. And sometimes, things you learn in one of your writing venues can benefit your writing in both venues. For example, knowing my overused words in my fiction makes me aware of when I'm overusing them in any context, which helps me to streamline writing I do for my day job (and helps me to edit other peoples' writing, too).

My day job is more editing than writing, so I don't feel like I'm doing too much of the same thing. When I do get a chance to write at work, it can actually be a nice change from normal. And the topics I'm writing on are much different from what I'm writing for fun, so it's easy to find a divide between the two.

If your day job is primarily writing, you might feel like you're using up all your words during the day and have none left for your fiction writing. If you're in this position, you might try doing some writing warm-up exercises to get the creative words flowing a little better. You may also find you need to schedule specific times to write, potentially before you start your day job writing, or on days when you don't need to write anything for your day job.

~

When Planning Goes Awry

I am a planner. I have spreadsheets and planner books and to-do lists keeping me on track with my writing. And though I adjust them all the time, I'm never without a plan.

However, a while back, I was scheduled for surgery on a specific date. In anticipation, I cleared my schedule for six weeks after the surgery, which was the estimated recovery time. I was planning to only get writing done if I felt like it, and then it would probably be poetry and maybe something short. But I was going to take it easy and not worry about not writing.

But then my surgery was postponed. Indefinitely (thanks to a COVID surge). "Indefinitely" is one of the worst words for someone who plans her schedule so thoroughly, because I could only make plans that might get disrupted at any minute. The surgery was not for a life-threatening matter, but it was still frustrating to make those plans and then have to be ready to readjust as soon as it could be rescheduled.

I knew if I left my calendar open, I'd get absolutely nothing done, though, so I had to come up with a backup plan. It wasn't my normal level of writing, but it was at least something resembling a schedule, which was enough to quiet the parts of my mind that don't like to be without a plan.

The surgery was eventually rescheduled, completed, and I recovered nicely. But the need to pivot from one plan to another was a challenge that slowed my progress. I had to remind myself it was only a speed bump, and I could and did get back on track once I was done recovering.

If you wind up in a situation where your planning has to be adjusted, remind yourself that it's a speed bump, not an insurmountable mountain. While it may slow you down temporarily, there are ways to pick your speed back up once you're past the speed bump, whatever it may be.

~

When Busy Turns to Juggling Knives

I often work on a lot of projects simultaneously, which occasionally shifts from being busy (my normal state) to a point I like to call "juggling knives." I use the phrase in the context of it being a dangerous thing, and it's something I have to be careful to watch out for, because for me, going beyond busy into "juggling knives" territory is a quick route to being overwhelmed and then burned out.

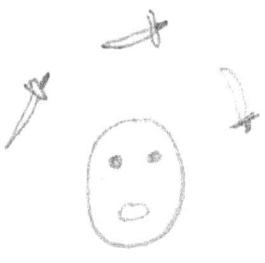

One of my tactics for dealing with juggling knives is making a lot of lists—more lists than normal, because as I get busier, my memory tends to lose track of things. So having lists means I can make sure everything gets done. I also start breaking out the lists by day. I already do a lot of scheduling based on days of the week, but as my busy-ness increases into larger projects, sometimes it's a matter of needing to set aside a specific chunk of time to knock one of those larger projects out. For me, knowing when I'll get around to doing something allows me to put it a little farther out of my mind, since I know I will be getting to it on the day I've scheduled it for.

I've also found a lot of value in keeping track of what I have done, as well as what I need to do. When there's a whole lot going on, I can spend a good chunk of a day working but feel like I haven't accomplished much because there are still so many things not done yet. By making a list of what I've gotten done, I have a visible way to remember "oh yeah, I did stuff."

Finally, sometimes I have to remind myself I don't have to do everything at the same time. I have few solid deadlines, and fewer externally imposed deadlines. There are some things I can move off my immediate priority list and onto a secondary priority list,[6] freeing up space (and brain power) for the more pressing items.

While you might not be working on multiple projects at once, there are plenty of other things getting in the way of your writing, causing complications. And no matter how much you plan, things don't always go the way you planned. Best laid plans of mice and men, something, something. Part of being a writer also means having the flexibility to adjust your schedule and your goals based on your personal reality. And while I can offer some tips and tricks that have worked for me, your mileage absolutely will vary.

~

---

[6] My main priority list is for things I'm actively working on. My secondary priority list is for things I plan to work on in the future. When I move something from the main list to the secondary list, I often call it "backburnering," as I've moved it out of my immediate reach and onto the back burner of the stove, as it were.

Writer's Block

Like most writers, there are days when I stare at the blank page, the cursor blinking at me, like it knows I have nothing to say to it. It's the dreaded writer's block, or at least the temporary shutdown of my brain that doesn't want to let me write. Since I try to write five days a week and have a lot of projects I'm trying to complete each week, a day of not getting much done can slow down the whole process. So I have some go-to activities bound to unlock my brain.

1. **Taking a shower/bath.** Why do people always get their best ideas when they're in a position where they can't do much about them? I can develop elaborate scenes and dialogue when I'm in the shower. I've considered getting a grease pencil for when good ideas strike me, but then I'd probably have a smudgy black wall in the shower. Or I'd wind up in there until the water runs cold. So maybe writing in the shower isn't the solution, but if it can get my brain unstuck AND I can get those ideas transferred to paper (or my phone, or the computer), it's a good technique to battle writer's block.

2. **Driving.** Again, driving is another situation involving being in a place where you can't do much writing. I'm in the unfortunate position of being one who gets carsick if I try to write or read (or use my phone) as a passenger, so even if I'm not the driver, I'm somewhat limited in what I can do while in the car. I've considered turning on the recorder on my phone and narrating my ideas as I go, but that's not necessarily a safe option. If I'm driving and my husband is there, I occasionally will ask him to take notes on his phone and email them to me, but that's usually only when we're on a long drive. Mostly, though, I end up thinking and rethinking the ideas, and then hope I can make it to paper (or the equivalent) before they escape.

3. **Cooking prep.** There's something rhythmic and slightly mindless about doing food prep, like chopping fruits and vegetables, or making a recipe you've made countless times before. (It's better to not try to make a recipe involving counting, as working on a plot and counting can cause all sorts of mix-ups.) Sometimes, when I've been stuck on a story, heading to the kitchen to do a little prep work can be the thing that jiggles the pieces loose

in my head. And unlike the previous two suggestions, some cooking prep is the sort of thing that could be paused while you hurry to scribble down an idea, so long as you're able to rinse the messy or smelly bits of food off your hands and not get them all over your paper or device.

4. **Doing something else.** Some days, I have to live with my inability to get writing done. Sometimes I can redirect things to working on business of writing things (like writing a blog post instead of fiction, for example), but other days, I have to accept it's a wash and do something completely different. Every once in a while, giving my brain a break is the thing it needs in order to return to productivity. Maybe I'll get something done later that day, or maybe it'll take me a whole day of doing something else, but the occasional breaks tend to be one of the better forces to fight writer's block. (And another reason why I don't try to make myself write daily.)

If you're feeling blocked in your writing, my first suggestion is to try doing something else for a bit, something to take your mind off what you're writing. Somewhere in the back of your brain, the puzzle of your story is probably still going to be there, ticking away. But by shifting your primary focus, you can let it go on as a "background process" (to use a bit of a computer metaphor). Sometimes intentionally not thinking about the problem helps you find a solution.

Another thing to consider when you feel like you've got writer's block is the reason why you're feeling blocked. Have you been trying to cram too much into your life? Have you been so busy you haven't gotten to relax? Are you feeling like whatever it is you're writing is more than you can handle? Taking some time to think about what's blocking you can also help you work past it.

Finally, if you're blocked on a specific project, you might need to let that project take a short timeout and work on something different. Sometimes, getting the words flowing on another project is all it takes to work past the block on the other project. Or perhaps you're not blocked, but there could be something about the blocked project making you feel that way.

~

But What If It's Burnout?

The flip side of what might feel like writer's block is burnout. If you're a highly productive writer (like me), you might wind up frequently giving yourself more than you can manage. This is closely related to what I talked about earlier about "juggling knives."

When I have a long weekend, I often give myself a sizable writing to-do list. Sometimes, that to-do list ends up being overwhelming. If I push myself to get it all done, by the end of it, I'll have burned myself out.

For me, there are a couple of solutions to this. The first is, of course, reworking my to-do list when it gets to the point of overwhelming. In order to do this, you have to get to know how much work is too much, and then take a step back. Like the meme says, "Pick your battles. No, that's too many battles. Put some back." (Replace "battles" with "projects". You get the idea.)

The other thing I do to keep from burning out is to give myself breaks when I have a bunch of things to work on. Often, these breaks are still in front of my computer (looking at social media or doing other non-writing computer tasks), so I also make myself get up every now and then and do something not involving looking at a screen. In a perfect world, some of those breaks are short walks outside, but that doesn't always wind up happening.

Sometimes, burnout can be more than overdoing it on the writing front. We all have complex lives with a lot of moving parts, some of us more than others. Even if the amount you're writing isn't overwhelming, you might be dealing with a hectic time at a day job, illness within your household or among your family or friends or pets, and myriad other things all demanding your attention. Our society puts such an emphasis on being productive, it's easy to get overwhelmed with all the things you need to do and want to do.

The most important thing to remember is to be kind to yourself. We are not machines, but even machines break down from overuse. We can too if we're not cautious. So while I am the biggest cheerleader for "you can do it! Write all the things!", I also encourage all writers to set a comfortable pace for you and forgive yourself if you need to relax your pace when life gets in the way. You don't have to write all the things right now. Spread them out at a pace that works for you. And maybe put some back for a little while.

Profit?

So, you've finished your novel.

Or have you?

Finishing writing the novel is only step one, unfortunately. If you want that novel out in the world so you can rake in the big bucks ...

(Raking in the big bucks is not guaranteed in the slightest. There are some novels that do, but the majority do not, sadly.)

So scaling down our plan a bit, if you want that novel out in the world (with no expectations of big bucks), there's still a bit more in the process.

Whether you decide to self-publish, publish with a small press, or pursue an agent and a book deal for your novel, you're going to want to revise it first. No matter how brilliant you're sure your novel is, please, please, please revise and edit it before sending it out to anyone other than your dearest friends and family, who you know will love your story no matter how messy.

Because your first draft? It's going to be messy. Take it from someone who does a lot of editing for experienced authors, it's going to be messy. (Even my own novel drafts are littered with typos and misused words, and I get paid to edit as my day job. Trust me on the messy.)

So before you can get to "Profit?", you're going to want to revise your novel. You might also want beta readers, sensitivity readers, an editor, and more. And then comes the whole agent-seeking process. Let's break all of that down.

~

Revisions: Making the Words Better

Revising a novel can be as individual as writing a novel. There are all sorts of options for how to go about it. Some authors may opt to read through their draft novel (either on the screen or printed out) and make notes within the electronic document, in a separate electronic document, in a notebook, or on the printed-out version (if you've done so). Others might do their revisions in phases, where they only look at one specific aspect of their novel, like characterization, dialogue, descriptions, etc., in each pass.

Revisions, much like your first draft, are messy. You may find yourself metaphorically ripping up entire sections of your novel and then putting those pieces back together. You may realize you've left out huge chunks that now need to be written. You may decide to remove the first three chapters, now that you've realized where the story actually starts.

When you begin revisions, save a copy of your first draft and hide it away in a folder. This is your insurance copy. If you accidentally delete a section during revisions, whether through a simple slip of the fingers or because you think you don't need it, it will not be forever lost because of your insurance copy.

In fact, I recommend saving a LOT of versions of your novel as you revise. Most primarily text documents don't take up much hard drive space, and it's far better to be able to find a copy of the brilliant bit you wrote, then discarded, and then realized you needed after all, than for it to be lost to the data void. (Yes, there are ways to recover old files, but you can make it a lot less stressful on yourself if you save early and save often.)

So what should you be revising? Like I said, this can be individual. When I write a novel, my descriptions are quite sparse in the first draft. This is because I see the scenes I'm writing in my mind, but those details don't always make it to the page. So when I'm revising, descriptions and details are some of the things I need to look for. Other aspects might be characterization, to make sure your characters behave consistently (unless the changes are part of their character arc) throughout the course of the novel. Dialogue, too, is something to look at, particularly the ways in which different characters speak, their word choices, their slang use, etc. And of course, you're also checking that the plot is coherent and makes sense, there aren't huge leaps of logic or skipping over significant plot points, and more.

It's a lot. It can take longer to revise a novel than it took you to write it. You might need to do multiple rounds of revisions. It can be harder to revise than it was to write.

But when you're revising, you do have the advantage of having already written a draft. Even if it requires a lot of work, the writing is the hardest part (even if it doesn't always seem that way). Without that draft, you've got nothing to revise.

~

How I Revise a Novel: The Revision Wall

When I sat down to revise *Promise Me Nothing*, I knew I had a bunch of subplots and seemingly insignificant things strewn throughout. I wanted a way to track all those things, to make sure I had followed all the threads to their natural conclusion.

To start my process, I looked at my original outline and compared it to the first draft, summarizing the major points of each scene. As I worked through this, I also identified places where I needed to expand things, places to put in some new subplots, and notes on where various subplots and other things appeared. I color coded some of these in my summary notes, assigning a random color to each piece as I identified it. I also flagged shorter than average chapters, so I could consider adding some of the new or expanded subplots there to bulk them up a bit.

Then I made a landscape-oriented page for each chapter of the novel, set up a table with the appropriate number of columns for each scene in that chapter, and put the summary notes into those columns. Most of my chapters had three scenes, so I lined up those three scenes into side-by-side columns and enlarged everything as big as I could make it and still fit onto a single page for each chapter.

Then I printed it all out, one page per chapter, and hung those pages in the corner of our guest bedroom (because it's the largest swath of unadorned wall in our apartment, and it's a room the cats, who see wall hangings as a toy, aren't allowed in). Then I could look at everything in a "big picture" sense and scribble notes on each sheet about the revisions I wanted to make. This was super useful for me to notice things like when a major character vanished about one-third of the way into the book or when a plot thread evaporated without being resolved. Both of those could then be scribbled onto the sheets for later chapters so I could keep that character around or wrap up that plot thread.

Then I took a photo of each of these sheets individually to refer to when I was at my computer. In that mode, I could see what I'd typed and what I'd handwritten, and that information gave me a blueprint for how to revise the chapters. And then I worked through them one by one.

You don't have to do this on individual sheets of paper. Some people use large post-it notes or index cards to the same effect. You also don't have to do this on physical items—there are programs that will let you do what I did digitally. For me, though, doing this physically let me consider everything in a different way, one I don't think I could have accomplished without having the revision wall.

The revision wall and breaking down each chapter like this also helped me find some errors, like having two Wednesdays in the same week. Weirdly, though my novel has all sorts of supernatural creatures, there weren't any who could make two Wednesdays in a week. (I mean, there could have been, but that would have been an entirely new subplot, and it wasn't one I wanted to add.)

Finally, the brief scene summaries I used are also a way to start writing a synopsis of the book, which I'll talk about more later.

~

Timing from Idea to Book

How long does it take between when an author gets an idea for a novel and when it comes out as a published book? That depends on a number of factors, including the author and their publication process. But the short answer is "longer than you'd think."

According to my various notes on each, *Promise Me Nothing* and *Barren* (a novella) took about five or six years from idea to publication. This seemed longer than I expected, so I looked at some of my other books.

Brass and Glass: The Cask of Cranglimmering similarly took about five years from idea to publication. The sequels in that series took less time, largely because they were sequels, and I wanted to keep the series fresh in peoples' minds. Still, we were in the early stages of getting the first *Brass and Glass* book into the world when my small-press publishers asked me about sequels, and I worked up the outlines for those. So *The Long-Cursed Map* (book 2) was about a year and a half in the works, while *The Boiling Sea* (book 3) took almost three years from idea to publication (though I was also writing book 2 during that period, and my original publisher closed when we were partway through the process on book 3, which extended how long it took to get the final book out).

For authors pursuing traditional publication, it may take even longer from when they start writing the book to the point where they 1) find an agent and 2) find an editor/publisher. And then it's more time before a book is published, as there are additional edits and proofreading and publicity all scheduled in advance of the book's release date. However, if they sell the first book in a series, and the editor/publisher wants additional books, they may have a similar compressed time frame like I did for my sequels.

Also, different people write at different speeds. When I'm writing a novel, I can finish the first draft in a little over two months. Then it takes another couple of months for me to make my initial edits to it. Then it goes out to beta readers for a month or two, and then there are more rounds of revisions, which can vary in number and length depending on what the book needs. It's theoretically possible for me to start a book on January 1st and have it self-published by the end of the year, but that's an unusual situation.

The takeaway from all of this is publishing takes a while, whether traditional, small press, or self-publishing. And while it may be agonizing to have to wait for your book to be ready for readers, putting in the time and effort to make your book great is important, no matter how you're publishing.

~

Beta Readers and Sensitivity Readers (and Why They're Usually Not the Same People)

I mentioned beta readers when talking about how long it takes to get a novel published. Who are these magical people? (And let me assure you, they are magical!)

Beta readers are the people who read your novel after you've done some revisions (please, do them a favor, and don't send them your raw, unrevised manuscript). They can give you insight into what works or does not work for them, things they loved, things they found confusing, and more. Basically, they're your audience before your book is ready for a full audience. Think of it like a sneak preview. (Only unlike a movie sneak preview, your book isn't completely done yet, which means you've got the chance to fix anything that's not quite working.)

The reason they're called beta readers is because they're second readers. You should be your own alpha reader, or first reader. As I said before, spare them the rough first draft and give them at least a revised draft.

Beta readers can be just about anyone. However, not all beta readers are created equal. When I've put out calls for beta readers for my books, many people will step up and ask me to send them a copy. Most of them, however, don't actually provide any feedback. Either their time gets away from them and they can't read the book by the deadline I gave them, or they forget I sent it to them. Or they feel like they can't offer me any helpful suggestions. (They're probably wrong on that last point.)

My best beta reader is my sister from another mister, one of my dearest friends. She's also trained as an editor, so she's a hawk-eyed beta reader. And she knows me well enough to know she can tell me exactly what's wrong with my novel and I won't be offended. (If I was going to be offended by suggestions, I'd say I was in the wrong line of work.)

So if you're looking for beta readers, think about your friends and family members who have writing or editing experience. If none of them do, find the most voracious readers. Because voracious readers, even if they don't write, will have opinions about what makes a good book. It can also be advisable to look for beta readers through writer's communities you're a part of.

However, I have two caveats here, the first of which also applies to anyone you ask to beta read for you. One, they should be familiar with your genre. If you're writing science fiction, your grandma who only reads romance novels, no matter how voraciously, is not a great beta reader for you. (She'll probably also tell you, "oh, it's perfect, sweetie," or whatever pet name she uses for you.) Beta readers from a writer's community should also be people familiar with your genre, for the same reason. (Though they probably don't call you sweetie.)

Second, if you are part of a writer's community and are asking for beta readers, you should also be offering to beta read for others. It should be a give and take relationship. Too many times, I see new folks show up to an online writer's community and immediately ask for beta readers. (When I see the same person show up in multiple places with the same request, I get extra wary.) Beta reading for other writers is a great way to learn more about writing, as you see what does and does not work for you. So though it will take up some of your precious time, it's good for your karma and good for your craft.

When you do seek out beta readers in any capacity, be sure to let them know what kind of feedback you're looking for. That feedback should include both the good and the bad, but you can also ask about specific aspects of your characters, plot, world building, setting, whatever.

Most beta readers are not looking at your book in terms of editing. My best beta reader will let me know if she spots an egregious typo, but she knows my books will be going through a full edit later, so she doesn't need to sweat the small stuff. Some beta readers might do the same, but you probably don't want a beta reader who is going to nitpick every error in still unedited (albeit revised) text.

Sensitivity readers are a different sort of reader. If you've written a novel with a diverse cast of characters, some of those characters possess qualities you yourself do not. These might be things like race, ethnicity, gender identity, sexuality, disability (physical or mental), body type, religion, family income, immigration status, and many, many more possibilities. When one of your primary characters is of a marginalized identity you do not share, it's time to consider a sensitivity reader.

Sensitivity readers should not be reading your book out of the kindness of their hearts. They should be getting paid for their labor. Full stop. Especially because they may be reading things that cause them emotional trauma (not because you are setting out to do so, but because we are all the products of our upbringing and circumstances, and we don't know what we don't know), they should absolutely, one hundred percent, be paid for their time and labor.

(Is barter an option with sensitivity readers? It can be, but you should never presume it will be, even if you establish an ongoing working relationship with a sensitivity reader. You should always expect to pay them, and you should make that clear when you reach out to them. However, you may ask if they would consider a barter arrangement, as long as you're prepared to accept no for an answer and be gracious about it.)

Not all sensitivity readers can or should read for all marginalized identities. For example, I'm a bisexual woman with mental health disabilities who was raised Catholic in a middle-class family. But I'm extremely White, fifth-generation American, don't have physical disabilities (aside from bad vision), and have never experienced extreme poverty and/or being unhoused. Could I be a sensitivity reader? Heck yeah.

But only for the things that are a part of my identity. I could be a sensitivity reader for your novel about a White woman growing up in the Catholic Church, for example. I could be a sensitivity reader for your novel about a bisexual woman growing up middle-class American.

But you should not be hiring me (or someone like me) as a sensitivity reader for your transfemme, Black, Baptist, first-generation immigrant character who uses a wheelchair. That's not my lived experience, and I shouldn't be considered an expert on those aspects of your character's life. But there are people out there who are, and they should be the people you seek out as sensitivity readers.

Sensitivity readers can come into play at various stages of your process. You can consult with a sensitivity reader before you've written anything, when your novel is just an idea, if you know it will contain aspects you might want to learn more about before you write it. You can also hire a sensitivity reader to look at an outline. You might send them your manuscript at the same time it goes to beta readers, or you may wait until it's closer to done. (Though don't wait too long in the process, in case they identify an issue requiring a lot of changes.)

I know some writers might read this bit of the book and say "I'm writing fantasy. This isn't relevant to me." It is, though. If you look back at the history of some of the classic fantasy tropes, there's a deep history of racism, sexism, and ableism in that genre. Or you might say "I'm writing science fiction that's post-race/-gender/-whatever." But as I mentioned above, you're still the product of a society in which racism, sexism, ableism, and more are factors in your upbringing and life, and those things are baked into your subconscious in ways you might not realize until someone points them out to you.

There are also some writers who might say, "oh, I only write characters who are exactly like me." And I really, really hope that isn't true, because that would likely be a pretty boring story. (There are arguments in the "stay in your lane" camp suggesting people shouldn't be writing marginalized characters when they don't share those marginalizations, but I think books are better when they include diverse characters who the author has done research and sought feedback on.)

So consider hiring a sensitivity reader, no matter what genre you're writing. In the best-case scenario, they may find nothing objectionable in what you've written. In the worst-case scenario, they may find things that require you to rethink your entire novel. But both of those (and everything in between) are far better than publishing something you're later ashamed of because you didn't hire a sensitivity reader.

~

Now, why shouldn't beta readers and sensitivity readers be the same people? I think you may already know the reason.

Beta readers don't get paid. Sensitivity readers do.

Does this mean you should never ask a marginalized person to be a beta reader? No. But it does mean you should respect that if you're not paying them for a sensitivity read, you shouldn't expect that level of labor from them. It also means if they find your book to be harmful for them or more emotional labor than they're prepared to do, they might not finish reading your book.

And it also means, if they do take the time to educate you on their marginalization, you should thank them profusely. You might offer to pay them, even if that wasn't part of your original agreement. You owe them. Big time.

~

Dealing with Feedback

When you get feedback, how do you deal with it?

First, remember the feedback is not about you as a person. It's about what you wrote. And it doesn't mean what you wrote isn't good. But it's easy to mistake feedback, especially negative feedback, as a reflection on you or your writing.

Not every piece is right for every person who reads it. As a reader, you've probably found books you didn't enjoy or books you never read because you were pretty sure you wouldn't enjoy them. Keeping this in mind when you receive feedback can be a valuable approach.

When feedback explains what didn't work for the reader, it's good insight, but it doesn't mean it's something that needs fixing. Readers don't always understand the story you're trying to tell. Sometimes it means your writing needs more clarity, other times it's a them thing.

Breaking this down a little further, the first sentence in the last paragraph is talking about the sort of feedback that gives suggestions for what the story needs or doesn't need. For example, feedback could say "I found this side character unimportant to the story." Some writers might see that suggestion and think "oh, I'll remove that character." But the important thing to remember is one person found the character unimportant. Unless you fully agree with their assessment, I'd leave the character alone.

There's also a difference between something being unclear vs. a reader not understanding it. Sometimes they're connected. But veteran writers have many stories about feedback that completely missed something they'd explicitly written. In some cases, there are revisions needed to make something clearer, but in other cases, the information is clear as day, and the reader missed it entirely.

So if there's a case where feedback mentions something you think is crystal clear as being missing, it can be worth it to take a step back and make sure the thing is as clear as you believe it to be. Maybe ask someone who hasn't already read it to look at it. However, it's also possible the reader who gave you that feedback missed what you wrote. So it doesn't always mean you need to revise that part.

The short version is: when you get feedback, consider what the reader is saying. You don't always have to act on their suggestions, but they may be worth at least considering closely to see if they are giving you advice to make your story better (period) or to make your story better for them. The first is worth doing, while the second sometimes is not.

It's also worth considering that if someone tells you something is wrong with your story, they may be correct. If someone tells you *how to fix it*, however, they may be incorrect. Because, in the end, it's your story, and part of what makes it your story is your writing.

~

Editing

Okay, you've done your revisions, you've had beta readers and/or sensitivity readers give you feedback, you've implemented the feedback (don't forget this step), and now it's time for some editing.

There are a lot of types of editing, which I'll talk more about below, but the main thing I want to talk about here is self-editing. If you're planning to self-publish your book, you probably will also want to hire a professional editor. But if you're planning to submit to indie presses or agents, it's likely sufficient for you to self-edit your book before sending it to those places, because they should put you through a more rigorous editing process as part of your path to publication.

But it's still a good idea to get your book as tidy as possible before sending it to an indie press or an agent. It's one thing to have a well-plotted book, but it's another thing to have a book that's generally clean on the grammar and punctuation. Sending a manuscript riddled with easily fixed errors generally doesn't make a good impression on indie presses and agents, so it's in your best interest to go through your book with a fine-toothed comb before sending it off.

You certainly can hire an editor to help with this part of the process, but editing costs money, and when you've got a novel manuscript that you don't know will sell, you may be reluctant to spend money on getting it edited. And that's completely fair. But at the same time, it is an option if you don't feel comfortable with your knowledge of grammar and punctuation rules. (And yes, authors are allowed to break some of those rules, but it's generally a good idea to understand the rules before you break them, so you can justify why you've done so.)

It's also valuable to self-edit a manuscript you plan to send to a professional editor as well. Why? Many (though not all) editors charge by the hour for editing. The more time and work your manuscript requires, the more expensive editing will be. So it's in your financial interest to do your best with preliminary self-editing before you hire a professional.

I've got a list of tips for self-editing I often share with writers to help them through the process. If you want to effectively spruce up your book before sending it out into the world, these tips will help.

Finish First: When I started writing, I would often go back to my first chapter or opening scene again and again and again. So I would have a lovely, polished opening scene, but I didn't necessarily finish what I was working on. Currently, when I'm working on a first draft of something, I try hard to not re-read much of what I've written in that piece previously, lest I fall into the trap of polishing before something is done. If I need to re-read, I resist the urge to poke at the text, unless I see something that's definitely wrong and needs to be fixed so it doesn't lead me astray later. But then, I need to get on with writing new words until I'm at the end of the first draft. Editing as you go may seem like it has the potential to be efficient, but it isn't, especially when it comes at the expense of finishing.

Give It Some Space: When you've finished a piece, it's a good idea to take some time away from it before you edit to give yourself a more objective eye. Many writers are their own worst critics, and tackling the editing on a piece you've recently finished may lead you to over-edit that finished piece. By taking some time away from your first draft, you'll allow yourself to come back to it with fresh eyes, so you might find you actually like what you wrote. The time also helps you to see errors more clearly, as you're not as emotionally invested in the piece—you can read it almost as if someone else wrote it. The amount of time you need to spend away from the piece can vary based on your personal preferences, your schedule, and the length of the piece. For me personally, I like to give myself a couple of months away from a novel or novella. If you can get that distance from your writing, your self-editing will be all the more effective.

Read Aloud: When I have the time, reading aloud is one of the most useful tools in my editing arsenal, whether I'm editing something of my own or something written by someone else. When I'm editing for my day job, if I come across a sentence that seems off to me, I'll often read it aloud, to help me find where the sentence breaks down. If you can do this reading aloud with another person, it can be extremely useful. Failing that, however, there are software options that will read your text back to you, often in a highly robotic way, which can also be useful, as the robot won't skip any words. For most editors, this reading aloud pass comes toward the end of an editing cycle, but I've found it can also be useful if I want to hear how something sounds, to see if it's taking the right shape for what I'm trying to do, while I'm revising or editing a draft.

Listen to Feedback: When your readers give you feedback, remember to take it into account if it resonates with you. Listen to what they say about, for example, flat characters, pacing problems, or confusing action sequences. While some of those may point toward things you can work on immediately, some may also point to things you can learn to improve in your writing. Flat characters might mean you need to edit your work with an eye toward differentiating characters through their dialogue and body language. Pacing problems could mean your writing is overly wordy or too sparse (depending on whether people think your story drags or rushes by). Confusing action sequences could mean the language you're using to describe the action needs careful attention to detail.

Be Wary of Software "Corrections": If you use Microsoft Word to write, you're familiar with the squiggly red lines and blue lines indicating typos and grammatical errors ... or do they? If you're writing British English, Word is going to hate every word

73

Americans don't use the letter "U" in (like honor/honour). If you're writing fantasy or sci-fi, the odds are good at least one name in your story isn't a "real" word according to Word. If you write anything approximating actual human dialogue, you enter the land of the squiggly blue lines that don't like contractions or people who don't speak in business English. Oh, and swearing. Word doesn't want you to offend your readers.

And that's exactly the problem with the "corrections" software offers up. The spelling and grammar checkers in most software are designed to help people write for business purposes. They're not meant to help fiction writers. If you're a fiction writer, and you accept the suggestions Word gives you, you'll likely end up with a grammatically accurate piece, but it will smother your authorial voice. You can certainly look at the suggestions Word makes, but don't accept them without evaluating them carefully.

Learn to Spot Passive Voice: Passive voice is, quite simply, putting the object before the subject. Another way of explaining this is you're putting the thing that is acted upon before the person doing the acting. And since character-driven fiction is what most editors and readers are looking for, passive voice weakens the impact of your writing. Would you rather read "The wall was punched by Joe" or "Joe punched the wall"? The second of these, in the active voice, is much more dynamic. You know right away who is doing the thing, followed by what they are doing, and to what object. Unless that wall has been established as a REALLY interesting wall prior to this sentence, no one cares that much about the wall. When you've got a sentence in which the person doing the thing isn't clear, that can also be a case of passive voice. I see this a lot in historical writing, where in some cases, authors don't want to say things like "The U.S. government removed Indigenous peoples from their land." So instead, they say "The Indigenous peoples were removed from their land." See, no clear "actor" doing the thing in that case.

So how do you spot passive voice in your writing? Some people will tell you to look for "was" and "were", but those verbs in and of themselves aren't necessarily bad. You know what is bad? "By zombies."

If you can add the two words "by zombies" to the end of your sentence, you've probably got some passive voice lurking. "The Indigenous peoples were removed from their land by zombies." Highly unlikely. And also passive. "Elizabeth Bennet was asked to dance by zombies." Probably not, but maybe in *Pride and Prejudice and Zombies*. Probably it's some other handsome chap. So tell us about him first. Unless you've got a good reason to conceal the actor(s), have them, you know, act.

Identify Overused and Crutch Words: Everybody's got them—those words that no matter how much you try, they still crop up in your writing. For me, it's the word "that." I did a search on a 40,000-word novella I wrote, and there were 500 uses of the word "that" before I'd edited it. Once I finished my editing pass for that specific word? About half as many. There were more that came out as I did more editing, of course.[7] Other frequently overused words are adverbs (I don't advocate for the removal of all adverbs, but I sometimes wind up with three "likely"s in quick succession, which means I'm overusing adverbs) and sensory words (it's not always necessary to say someone heard or smelled or saw something, but rather you can describe the sound or smell or sight). Other authors may have different crutch words.

---

[7] Fun fact: at the moment I'm writing this footnote, this manuscript currently has exactly 700 uses of the word "that." (Well, 701 now.) A few hours later ... Now it's got 427. There were way too many before!

An easy way to identify your crutch words is to have a computer read you a piece of your writing, but only listen for repetition. What are the words that come up frequently? Jot them down and see if you can find ways to replace them with other words (but don't worry too much about words like "a," "the," most prepositions, and "say/said"). Keep a list of those words, because odds are you'll see them pop up in future pieces as well, until you finally train yourself out of their use. Or maybe you won't ever get completely away from them, as my "that" example above illustrates. But knowing those words are present in your writing and to look for them when you're editing can help your writing be smoother and less repetitive.

Figure Out Punctuation: Punctuation is one of the most difficult parts of grammar, and different punctuation marks have varying levels of difficulty. The comma, for example, is THE single most difficult mark of punctuation to master. This is the sort of specialized training editors have, and they can help you sort out your commas. But there are also easy to learn conventional uses of punctuation that authors should master. This can be things like how to punctuate dialogue correctly, or the difference between en dashes and em dashes. It's the sort of thing that takes some reading and comprehending the details of how these things are used, but doing so will impress editors who are considering your work, so it's useful to learn.

You can find a lot of guides to punctuation online, or you can go old school and find yourself a style guide like the *Chicago Manual of Style* or *The Elements of Style*. While again, some of what these guides focus on is business, academic, or journalistic writing, there are useful punctuation (and grammar) tips for fiction writers as well.

~

The Types of Editing

There are a lot of people in the world with the title "editor," but not all of them do the same thing. Here's a list of the types of editors you might encounter and what they can do for you.

Acquisitions editing is the process of selecting works for publication. In the novel world, this is what editors at publishers do as they read manuscripts they've received and decide which ones their publisher would like to acquire. In the short fiction and poetry world, this is also the task of an editor, who may have assistance to select the pieces a magazine or anthology or website will publish. In general, this is not something people can do for themselves, and it's not something you want to pay someone to do for you.

Developmental editing is looking at the overall structure, themes, and flow of a piece (novel or shorter) and ensuring everything fits together nicely. It's about getting rid of things that aren't working as hoped, revising things to make them work better in the greater whole, and adding things that are needed to make everything work together. This is a "big picture" kind of editing that looks more at structure than at the "nit-picky" details that come in later stages of editing.

Line editing is about working with a piece at the sentence level to make sure every sentence (and, in fact, every word) is doing its job well. This is about smoothing out writing at a finer level of detail than developmental editing would cover, but it's also looking at themes and flow. It can focus on getting dialogue from the various characters to be distinct and appropriate for each character. It can change the way sentences flow from one to the next. It's mostly about language, as distinct from grammar.

Copy editing is looking at the "nit-picky" details of grammar, punctuation, spelling, and consistency. This is what makes sure your secondary characters don't have one name at the beginning of a piece and a different name at the end (unless the story is about this name change). This is about making sure you haven't accidentally used a homonym instead of the correct word, your sentences are grammatically correct, and all the words are spelled correctly. This is the meat and potatoes of what I do as an editor in my day job (though I also do line editing, and a tiny bit of what could be called developmental editing for non-fiction).

Finally, **proofreading** is a lot like copy editing, only it relates to the actual "proof" copies of a (typically) printed work. This is where someone makes sure all the previous edits have been maintained throughout, and nothing has been missed, omitted, or added. While some people proofread the digital copy of the text prior to layout, it's always a good idea to give the layout a look as well. I know of one book that went to press without its first sentence, and my own original printing of *Brass and Glass 2* added several sections from book 1 to the text, so that look at the laid-out book is also a VERY important step in the editing process.

~

Synopses and Blurbs and Cover Letters, Oh My!

If you're planning to shop your novel around to indie presses or agents, you're going to need a synopsis, a blurb, and a cover letter. I'll explain each of these in turn, but for the moment: synopses. Even if you plan to self-publish, learning a little about how to write a synopsis can be useful.

There are a ton of different approaches to writing a synopsis, and you can find many of those online. Sometimes, you can find things to help you write a synopsis in guides to writing outlines, too.

The simplest method of writing a synopsis is to start by writing a sentence or two about what happens in each chapter of your book. You want to distill this down to the most important bits of each chapter. You don't need to mention every single character or every single awesome detail, but you do want to hit the high notes.

And you need to include all the chapters, even the ending. A synopsis is not a place to be coy about your plot twists and conclusion. The people who are reading your synopsis want to know the details, because those details help them determine if 1) your book has a fully realized plot and 2) your book has a fully realized ending.

When you've got all those sentences, you're going to have a pretty bland synopsis, with a lot of "this thing happens" and "then this other thing happens." Now is when you want to wordsmith the heck out of those bland sentences and make them compelling. Don't lie or embroider the truth, but give the sentences more action and excitement. Focus on the natural evolution of the plot: because this thing happens, then this other thing happens. At the same time, keep your character arc(s) in mind, and make sure those make an appearance as well.

Once you've done some wordsmithing, it's time to do a bit of editing and polishing to make everything flow beautifully and entice the folks reading it to wanting to read your novel.

I'm not going to lie. It's a lot of work to craft a compelling synopsis. I'm not entirely sure I've fully figured it out. But if you want to practice writing synopses before you get around to writing one for your novel, you can try your hand at writing a synopsis for your favorite movie. Think of each scene of the movie as a chapter and summarize each scene with a sentence or two. Then play around with what you've written to make it as compelling as you can.

If you want to test your skills, send it to some friends or family members without telling them what it's a synopsis of, and ask them to guess. (If you've used character names, and those character names end up being unique, it may give away the game a little too quickly. I mean, I don't think I'm going to fool anyone with a synopsis of *The Princess Bride* after the moment I've introduced Westley and Buttercup. And definitely not after I mention Prince Humperdink. Some names are a little too unique. But you could use stand-in names for the characters if you want to make your friends or family members guess without those sorts of clues.)

When it comes to writing the synopsis for your novel, you're going to want to write and revise quite a bit. Getting feedback from other authors on your synopsis can be painful, but especially if you know traditionally published authors who have been through this process before, their feedback can be invaluable. But other authors, whether traditionally published or not, will likely still understand the basics of what's needed for a synopsis and should be able to help with some fine tuning of your synopsis.

~

Do Self-Published Authors Need a Synopsis?

The answer to this question is ostensibly a simple no. But can it be valuable to attempt writing a synopsis, even if you don't need it? Yes.

One of the things I realized when I was working on the synopsis for *Promise Me Nothing* (which wound up being self-published) was it's a fantastic way to find all those plot holes still hanging out in your manuscript. When you break down all the things that happen in the novel, you realize if you've left plot threads hanging, if something never got explained, and if you have the same day of the week happen twice (oops).

In some ways, having a synopsis in mind when you're writing could help you avoid some of these pitfalls, but I feel like it might also stifle any new ideas from coming up during the writing. But it could be helpful if you're part of the way through a novel you feel like you're floundering with. If you write a synopsis of what's happened thus far and then work out what needs to happen to reach the ending you want, you might figure out what needs to come next. In this way, a synopsis could be an after-the-fact outline for pantsers. But it can also help plotters who may have discovered a problem with their original outline once they started writing. So there's a lot of utility to working with a synopsis, even if you don't plan to send your manuscript to agents or a small press.

~

Blurbs

While synopses might only be used for submission to agents and small presses, everyone needs a blurb.

The blurb is the back of the book text (or, in this age of digital publishing, the bit on bookseller sites that sums up the book and compels people to buy it). Some might call it an elevator pitch, but in my experience, a blurb is longer than most elevator pitches and offers more detail. So while the elevator pitch for *Brass and Glass: The Cask of Cranglimmering* might be as simple as "a crew of airship pirates hunt for a cask of legendary whiskey and stumble across a more valuable secret," the actual blurb is considerably longer, to the tune of a tag line and a long paragraph of summary.

While a synopsis covers all the details of your plot, including the resolution, a blurb is going to be coyer, mainly giving the setup for the problem your characters face. Simply put, synopses have spoilers, blurbs do not.

Writing blurbs is another place where practicing with a favorite movie can be useful. Rather than writing out all the details of the plot, think about the basic problem the characters are faced with. You might include some additional complications if they don't give away too much of the plot, but the goal for a blurb is to keep it short and get it to compel those who read it to want to know more.

It's also important for your blurb to not be misleading. If you're writing a romance novel, make sure the blurb makes that clear. There's nothing worse than picking up a book based on the blurb, only to discover the blurb made the book sound different than what it is. For example, imagine if the blurb for *Twilight* made it sound like a gritty horror novel with terrifying vampires. Those readers who bought the book hoping for those vampires are going to be disappointed to find out the vampires sparkle and aren't all that terrifying.

It can be helpful to browse any major bookseller site for other books in your genre to get an idea of the conventions of writing a blurb for that genre. You may find some outliers, but by and large, you'll get a sense of how authors (or publicists) in that genre craft their blurbs.

If your book is chosen for traditional or small-press publishing, you'll likely get some help with crafting your blurb. But it is a useful skill to possess, and it's essential for self-publishing.

Much like with synopses, getting other folks to read your blurb can be incredibly useful. You can write more than one blurb and see which one people prefer. If you can get them to tell you why they prefer it, that's valuable insight on how to improve your blurb-writing skills.

~

Cover Letters

If you plan on shooting for traditional or small-press publishing, you may also need a cover letter for your submission. The cover letter is its own beast, where you give a little information about your book, comparable books ("comps"), and yourself. The information you need about your book is something sort of halfway in between a tag line, elevator pitch, and blurb. It's meant to be "hook-y" and entice the agent or publisher to want to know more.

Probably the part of cover letters that cause authors the most grief is the comps. None of us want to think our book is the same as someone else's book. But publishers want to acquire new books that are close enough to something recent with a good track record of sales.

The problem, of course, is finding those books. If you're widely read in your genre and have somehow kept up to date with the new releases while you've been writing and revising your novel, you're at an advantage. But for me, at least, it's hard to read other books in my genre while I'm writing and revising. My brain is too much of a sponge that soaks up the media I take in. So if I'm reading a bunch of young adult books while writing a young adult book, I'm going to inadvertently borrow way too much from those other books.

Comps can also be difficult to find for marginalized writers who are writing "own voices" novels, simply because there might not be anything like their novel out there. And some authors take their inspirations from non-novel media, like graphic novels, comic books, movies, or TV.

Some agents today are more willing to consider books without comps, or with non-novel comps, but by and large, if you're going to pitch a book, you're probably going to want comps to include in your cover letter.

In terms of what you need to say about yourself, you can talk about things that make sense given the subject matter of your book, other publications you have, and your social media accounts. These are all things a potential agent or small press is interested in for the purposes of marketing your work. As much as you may not like the idea of talking about yourself, it's essential here.

Because ultimately, what agents and small presses want out of a cover letter is "ways to get people excited about your book." The more you can give them (within reason—you don't need to go overboard here), the more they can work with.

~

Backwards and In High Heels: Doing It When Things Are Hard[8]

While the preceding sections of this chapter tell you a bit about how to go from idea to draft and from draft to something to send out or self-publish, the information isn't universal. It assumes you're in a position where you can take time out of your day to write, revise, and otherwise create a novel. It also assumes your body will allow you to sit at a keyboard for stretches of time. It assumes, in many ways, most of your basic needs are taken care of.

And that's not the case for all writers.

While I can't personally speak to every situation a writer might find themselves in, I can acknowledge my assumptions in writing this. Much of the advice I've given assumes you have a computer and access to the internet. It assumes you're not a person with a disability, physical or mental, that makes reading or writing difficult. It assumes you don't have financial, employment, or housing stressors preventing you from writing. It also doesn't get anywhere into cultural, ethnic, racial, religious, or other social impacts to your ability to take time for yourself to write.

All this is to say that my advice, like most writing advice, should be taken with a grain of salt and with consideration for your own unique circumstances. If something I've said is not possible for you to fathom, that's okay. It doesn't mean you can't be a writer or write a novel.

~

Working within Limitations

As I've gotten older, I've discovered I have physical, mental, and emotional limitations that either weren't there when I was younger, or that I had the energy to work around or the sheer bullheadedness to push through (hello, yes, I am an Aries, why do you ask?). However it worked then, it doesn't work the same now,

---

[8] Hat tip to Ginger Rogers, who did everything Fred Astaire did, backwards and in high heels.

and I've had to learn to acknowledge my limitations and find new ways to work around them.

Different illnesses and/or disabilities (physical, mental, and otherwise) can impact writers in different ways, and it can be difficult to feel like you're falling behind while others are soaring forward. But for me, pushing through and forcing myself to do EVERYTHING winds up leaving me exhausted and broken by the end of it. So I have to pace myself more carefully and look at the larger picture, not only at what's on my plate right this minute.

Sometimes that means rearranging my writing schedule to give myself more time to finish something that seemed like it could be done more quickly. And sometimes it means cancelling plans to give myself the time I need to finish another thing. Sometimes that includes cancelling plans early during a weekend so I can (hopefully) maintain enough energy to get through to something we've got planned for later. It's a careful balancing act, and it doesn't always work out as planned, but it's important for me to see those limitations, anticipate how they're likely to impact me, and plan accordingly.

If you've got similar limitations (or different limitations that affect you in similar ways), it's important to remind yourself of this sometimes. In many ways, this writing gig is a marathon, not a sprint, and sometimes looking at it in the long term and figuring out how that will work for you is key to moving forward.

~

Productivity during Stressful Times

In 2020, the world went topsy-turvy. We went into lockdown, a term most of us had never considered before, and we largely stayed home. For me personally, it meant a fast pivot from working in the office daily to working from home, a luxury my specific position within the company had never provided before. But with working from home came juggling the needs of two adults working in the same small space. And when we finished our workdays, we were still in the same space we'd been in all day.

This also meant our writing group, which had met twice a week previously, stopped meeting. We were on our own to get writing done, if we chose to do that. Or we could watch TV shows we'd gotten behind on, catch up on movies, read books, or whatever.

For a lot of authors, writing became hard, if not impossible. Anxiety was everywhere you looked. And as the lockdown dragged on, it became more and more difficult for people who craved social interaction. We did some video conferencing and meals in our friends' yard where we sat six or more feet away during pleasant weather. But it wasn't the same.

It's still not the same for a good many people. There are a lot of vulnerable populations who have not returned to "normal." And for those who have ostensibly returned to normal, there are still changes in our lives and behavior. And there's still a lot of stress and anxiety.

Sometimes, like in this instance, stressful times force us to take a break from our normal routine. Some can continue writing as normal or write more than they had been. Others feel the well of words dry up, leaving them staring at a blank page.

It's completely reasonable to slow down or shut down when outside stressors overwhelm you. And there are people for whom outside stressors are a constant thing. What's most important to remember during stressful times is to take care of yourself first. (If you have other people in your life who need your help, the same applies. If you aren't taking care of yourself, you aren't going to remain in a position to take care of others, either. It's why they tell you to put on your own life vest and/or oxygen mask in the event of a plane crash. You can't help other people if you're not floating and/or breathing.)

If that means not writing, so be it. If that means you can only write one sentence a day, it's one sentence more than you had before, and those will add up.

Yes, it's possible stressful times are your constant normal, and you don't see an end to the factors making your life stressful. But the same advice applies. Take care of yourself first, and do what you can manage, one bit at a time.

~

Tips for NaNoWriMo

A lot of people get into novel writing through NaNoWriMo.[9] Who doesn't want to write 50,000 words of a novel in thirty days? If that's you, or if you're considering doing it, here's a bit of advice I've accumulated through many years of NaNo.

NOVEMBER 2024						
					1	2
3	4	5	6	7	8	9
10	11	12	13	14	15	16
17	18	19	20	21	22	23
24	25	26	27	28	29	30

---

[9] It's worth noting that at the time of this writing, the organization that runs NaNoWriMo has been in considerable disarray. I'm not going to go into all the details here. Suffice it to say that a number of what were previously NaNoWriMo communities are stepping away from the organization, though they still plan to support authors writing in November. If writing a novel in the month of November is a thing you're interested in, you can do it through NaNoWriMo, with a local writing community (that may have formed out of previous NaNoWriMo participation), or by yourself.

Pre-plan. You're going to need a plan to get through writing 50,000 words in thirty days. I recommend an outline. If you're allergic to outlines, at least have a rough sketch in your head of what the big conflict of your novel is. Going into writing a novel without a plan can result in cool stuff, but having a plan in advance helps when you get stuck and guides you toward having something useful when the month is over.

Write ahead. No, I'm not advocating writing words before November 1 and counting them toward your goal (that's generally seen as cheating in the NaNo world). I'm suggesting if you have time to exceed the word count needed on a given day, do it. You never know what life is going to throw at you toward the end of the month. If common wisdom says you need to write 1,667 words a day, shoot for 2,000 words a day. That way, you can build up a buffer in case you can't write one day. It also prevents you from needing 10,000 words in the last three days of the month. (Yes, I've seen that happen, and I've seen someone win after being in that position. But it wasn't easy.)

Finish. This is a two-fold bit of advice. The first is you've got to try to get through your 50,000 words. But the likelihood is you won't have finished a novel in 50,000 words. And maybe you'll be burned out at the end of November. (Let's be honest. You WILL be burned out.) But you've still got to finish the novel if you ever want to do anything with it. So let it sit, but finish it, sooner rather than later. Try to get the same urgency as you had while doing NaNoWriMo to keep yourself generating new words until it's done.

Even if you don't "win," you're still a winner! While the official "win condition" for NaNoWriMo is writing 50,000 words, in my opinion, if you end November with 500 more words than you had at the beginning of November, you're still a winner, because you wrote words.

CHAPTER TWO: EXCUSES: HOW YOUR NOVEL CAN'T POSSIBLY GET WRITTEN

―――――――

I've said a lot about how to write a novel, and I've talked a bit about limitations that might make writing a novel more difficult.

But have you considered all those other things that get in the way of writing a novel?

Life throws so much at people, it's a wonder any of us are functioning as humans and writing. We've got our own inconstant meat sacks (a.k.a. our bodies), plus there are other people and beings in our life who need our time and energy.

Outside of that, distractions abound. It's easy to sit down after a long day and play games on your phone or computer or console, watch TV or movies or YouTube videos or TikToks, or do whatever else the internet has to offer. It's much harder to sit down and write.

This chapter doesn't have a lot of solutions or advice, at least not for most of it. It's a lot of grousing about things we can't control. But stick around until the end, because I do have a bit to say about things that are arguably "distractions" but can also be tools.

~

Have You Checked Your (Pet's) Butthole?[1]

I have cats. Two of them at present. They're rambunctious brothers. And they LOVE getting between me and my computer screen. One of them has an extra love of getting between me and my computer screen when I'm on a work video conference and showing off his butthole. Thankfully, my co-workers are mostly pet people too, so they're used to it. But man, does that cat love to show off his backside.

I'm pretty sure my cats don't want me to write. Seeing as they also don't like it when I play games on my phone, it's probably they don't like it when I'm doing something involving my hands that isn't petting them.

I hear dogs do this too. I'm not sure, because the two dogs I've spent any amount of time with either hide from my cats because they are a tiny chihuahua with a massive fear of cats, or they lay on the floor and give long-suffering sighs because we're inside and there's nothing for them to eat that they shouldn't. I get the impression this is not a statistically significant sample of dogs.

I don't know much about other pets, either. Fish are probably mostly harmless when it comes to getting writing done, though I am reminded of a fish my sister had that liked to leap from its tank. Birds, I think, are kind of jerks, but a lot of them live in cages, so

---

[1] Thanks, Tom Cardy!

they're maybe less jerks than my friend's bird who insists on sitting on or near him and shrieking when said bird is not getting enough attention.

So yeah, pets in general seem to be furry (or otherwise) assholes who don't want you to write.

I don't have a solution for this. Sometimes I trick my cats into leaving me alone by giving them something else to do. That lasts maybe ten or fifteen minutes, and then they're back again, wanting a lap and to be petted. Until they don't. And then they do again. So indecisive.

And you can't reason with them, either. They don't understand when you ask them to give you five or ten or fifteen more minutes, because what is time to them? I mean, one of my cats might understand that food goes on the plate at roughly 7:30 p.m., and if it's 8:00 p.m. and his humans are still staring at their screens, maybe he should make some noise about it, but he's smarter than the average cat, I'm pretty sure.

Anyway, what are you going to do? We have pets because we love them, even if they are assholes with a propensity for showing off their ... gonna stick with buttholes here. I can tell my cats they have to let me work because I'm the one who buys their food, but I can't claim my writing is paying for their food.

So I guess maybe pet them or something and then hope they decide to go do something different. Or maybe create an elaborate computer setup so they can sit on your lap when you write? Or at least nearby? (I have friends who have had some luck with putting a box on their desk for their cat to sit in, which makes the cat feel like they're a part of the action.) Your mileage may vary, especially if your pet is a lanky dog the same size as a smaller adult human, who doesn't fit on your lap.

Or a fish. You probably don't want your fish in your lap. Or to pet it.

~

Those Humans in Your Life Who Need Things from You

Oh, humans. Such fickle beings. Filled with needs.

Um, I mean, I'm definitely human too.

Not only do our own bodies need things like sustenance and rest, but oftentimes, we live with other humans who also need these things and more. And sometimes, those humans and their needs get in the way of our writing.

I'm not advocating for shunning human society and becoming a hermit (though I have pondered this option now and then). As it turns out, humans are social creatures, and even the most introverted among us probably needs at least some human contact. And, unfortunately, we aren't always able to control the frequency and length of such contact when we live with other people.

There are ways to set boundaries, sure. If you're lucky, you might have a door to close, from which you can hang a "Do Not Disturb" sign. If you don't have a door, maybe you've got headphones.

But while those are great ways to get some time to yourself to write, we don't always have that luxury. Some days, I tell myself I'm going to write between X and Y times, and then, as it turns out, my husband needs something from me during those hours. It might not take all the time, but it can still throw off my plans. And I get the impression that if you've got more members of your household, their needs for your time increase exponentially.

While people and their needs are a definite distraction, I suspect most of us who live with other people do so because we enjoy those people in our lives. Or, at the very least, there's some sort of mutual need being fulfilled. So it makes sense we would be willing to put our writing aside for them.

If you live with other adults, clear communication about your own needs in order to get writing done is important. If you live with children, that can be more difficult. Especially because the younger the child, the less likely they are to understand why they are not your focus. I mean, most babies don't understand human speech at all, which can be kind of frustrating when you tell them you want to sit and write for a bit.

So depending on the humans in your life, you may need to find ways to work around their needs in order to get the time you need to write. And I don't have much advice for this, either, especially not when it comes to babies. (My solution for babies has pretty much always been to hold them while they're happy and give them back to their parents when they aren't. That doesn't work as well when you are the parent.)

Even if you are in a position where you've got an understanding with the people you live with about writing time and not being disturbed, that tends to work only when you're in a standard routine. Sometimes, you get house guests or other disruptions to your normal.

The only thing I can say about those disruptions is sometimes you have to roll with them. When we have house guests, we might end up going places or doing non-writing activities at home with them. And I try to remember, as I'm "neglecting" my writing, I'm refilling the well where the words come from while I'm doing these other things, and that's important too.

So, yeah. People are people, and they'll get in your way, but they'll also give you ideas. So I guess it's a win in the end, even if it doesn't seem like it when they ask if they can ask you a question right when you're in the zone, and then suddenly you aren't in the zone, so you guess they might as well ask that question.

~

Your House Has Never Been Cleaner, You Must Be Writing a Novel

Are you the sort of person who would rather do anything than clean?

What about when your choices are clean or write?

A lot of authors say when they're struggling to get through a tough scene or part of their book, their living spaces are suddenly spotless, as they channel all their focus into cleaning instead of writing.

For me, I'm much happier writing than cleaning. But when it comes to revising ... oh, hey, look at that formerly cluttered table! Maybe it's time to clear off the bed in the spare room, in case someone wants to come visit. And so on.

There's something to be said for having a tidy space to work in, but it's also easy to go way overboard on the formerly dreaded cleaning when suddenly you would rather do anything than write or revise. So yes, it might be an improvement, but it's likely it didn't get you any words. Unless ...

Remember what I said back in the bit on writer's block? Where I talked about some of the methods I use to get unstuck? Cleaning might also be a way to take your mind off what you're working on enough to let your brain spin its wheels on the problem at hand. Even if you're not directly thinking about your novel, whether it's new words or revised words you need, shifting your focus can help you eventually get the solution you need.

That being said, cleaning everything is still a major distraction. It might be a sign you need a break from what you're doing, but it can also be a sign you're procrastinating. So it's worth evaluating why you've decided now is the moment when you want to pull all of the spices out of the cupboard, put them into new containers, and alphabetize them.

I've talked previously about using timers for writing, which is a thing I do quite often, either with a literal timer, with a group where we've designated specific times for writing and socializing, or with sprint bots on Discord. Timers can also be useful if you decide you need to take a short break from writing, whether it's to get out of your chair and move your body or to work on a specific, discrete project (like alphabetizing the spice cabinet). Call it Pomodoros or whatever else you like, but giving yourself a break from writing to clean (or do whatever else) isn't always a distraction, so long as you make sure to get back to the writing as soon as the other thing is done.

~

Distractions That Are Also Tools (Yes, They Exist)

Most of the time, if you should be writing, but you're doing something different, it's a distraction. However, there are some distractions that can be tools as well.

Back in the pre-pandemic days, one of my co-workers brought in a puzzle.

This, of course, escalated into a STACK of puzzles in the office. At one point, we did a swap with one of our other locations, where we each sent the other office the puzzles we'd already done, so we both had new-to-us puzzle variety. There was a thrift store run for puzzles in there too, somewhere, though I don't know who was responsible for it.

Most folks in my office used a portion of their lunch break to work on the puzzles, but every once in a while, when someone needed a mental break, either to step away from their project for a bit or to change gears before tackling another project, they'd work on the currently in-progress puzzle.

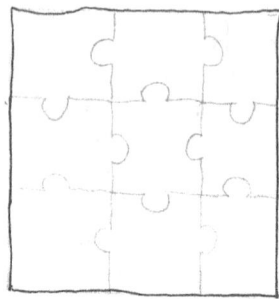

This sort of distraction can be a tool when you need a mental break for a story problem too. If you find yourself getting stuck, try finding another activity that still engages your brain but isn't writing. It could be a puzzle, but it could also be crosswords, sudoku, or word-related games. Anything that doesn't involve plotting or putting new words into your document is likely the best bet.

The process of engaging a different portion of your brain than you were using will sometimes let you shake loose the things keeping you from the solution to your story problem.

~

Writing Play

While writing practice is important to improving craft, writing play is also important to include in your routine. To me, the idea of writing play is that not every word you commit to paper (virtual or otherwise) will be publishable or usable. Sometimes, it's important to write things for fun—to play with words.

Writing play can be used to get "unstuck" from a problem with your plot, when you take a few minutes to write the LEAST likely way for the problem to resolve itself. By giving yourself the freedom to be utterly ridiculous for a brief period of time, you may find your way out of the corner into which you thought you had written yourself.

Writing play can also be a warm-up exercise for more serious writing, something to do if you don't have any other writing projects in mind at a given time, or something to fill a bit of time while you're waiting for something else. You can use writing prompts you've found in the wild or writing prompts you've written down for yourself.

Writing play can be a hard thing to do when you've got things you want to get done, and it's especially hard if, like me, you often take on a lot at any given time.

I've discovered it's important, though, to sometimes let myself play around with words. Maybe what I write in one of these writing play sessions will turn into a future project, but at the outset, the idea is to have fun with words and see what happens when you do so.

Sometimes, for me, writing play looks like going through some poems I've written that hadn't quite panned out as I hoped. When I've done this, I often identify some lovely gems hiding amidst the rubble. So I pull them out, write them on paper, and look at them with fresh eyes. Maybe I'll find something there. Maybe I'll take multiple ideas from different poems and find a way to mash them together. But pulling them out and looking at them with the intent to remind myself of what's there lets me see them through a different lens.

It's also relaxing to poke at something without a goal for it. Maybe it will end up being a page of scribbles in my notebook. Maybe it'll be years before I come back to it and realize something completely different than what Current Me would see in those words. Maybe those words will never see the light of day outside of my notebook.

And all of these maybes (and likely dozens more) are perfectly fine options when you engage in writing play. Let the play refresh you and lift some of your stress.

While many authors hope to make a career out of their words, that doesn't mean every word they write has to be directly related to that career. Any words you write, even in a spirit of play, will help you improve and expand your writing abilities.

And then you can get back to the stuff that needs to be done.

~

Playing with Writing

There are also games that let you play with writing. One variety of these is called lonely games, sometimes also called solo RPGs. The idea of a lonely game is a simple game you can play solo.[2] But, as it turns out, some of them can also make neat writing prompts.

The lonely games I prefer start with a statement, followed by a bit of setting, though you can always come up with your own setting if you prefer. Once you've had a moment to think about your story in terms of the statement, there are then a series of questions. For each question, you can take about five minutes to write. You can go for longer than five minutes on a question and then catch up to the other ones later, but I find when I've used a lonely game as a writing prompt, I generally reach a point where I'm ready for a new twist after about five minutes. (Bear in mind, too, I am a fast typist, so I can manage a lot of words in five minutes.) Finally, at the end of the questions, there's another statement, and you can spend a couple of minutes on that one.

And at the end? You'll probably have the bones of a story. It will need some fleshing out in places, and you may need to rearrange some of the pieces to make them fit together better. But you can easily wind up with the bones of a story in forty-five minutes or so, which is pretty darn good, especially for a story you have no ideas at all about before you start writing the first line.

---

[2] You can find lonely games by searching those words on sites like DriveThruRPG or itch.io. If you do a more general search, be sure to put them in quotes, as otherwise you get a whole bunch of games to play when you're lonely. My favorite lonely games are included in a collection called Of the Woods, which contains six different lonely games that make excellent writing prompts. I'm not certain every lonely game will work as a writing prompt, so you may want to check the details of any you're considering purchasing. You can likely find reviews of many of these lonely games online to learn more about them before you buy. The good news is most of them are quite inexpensive for a digital version of the game (many are only available digitally), with some being pay-what-you-can.

In the context of writing a novel, this sort of writing game might not be something that fits into your plot, but it might let you play with ideas for your characters, setting, world building, or other aspects you haven't thought about. It can also be a great way to get a bit of "stretching" in before turning to your actual project. Even if you only work through one question as a warm-up before turning to your main project, it can help you get your brain working and words flowing.

~

The Weird Stuff

Sometimes, it's not so much a distraction you need as a change of scenery, so to speak.

I don't mean running off into the woods with your laptop and writing there. Unless that works for you. (Wouldn't work for me. The woods are often damp and dirty, and there's nowhere to plug in my laptop.)

But there are things you can try that are different from your normal routine and you might find are more productive for you. It might involve writing while lying down or standing up or sitting cross-legged on the floor. It might involve changing the font or text color or size in your word processing program. You might need to give yourself a totally boring wall to look at, or you might need images (maybe related to what you're writing) in your space. You might want to pace and dictate to your phone or laptop. You might set up a treadmill so you can walk while you write.

There are a lot of possibilities for ways to get the words flowing, and they're not the same for everyone. It's worth taking some time to play with different ways of writing to figure out what works best for you. And it's not a distraction to try new things, so long as you recognize when the thing isn't working and move on to another option.

CHAPTER THREE: HOW TO TRICK YOURSELF INTO WRITING A NOVEL

If you, like me, require motivation to do pretty much anything, you're going to love this chapter. It's all about how to trick yourself into writing a novel by rewarding yourself. Sometimes, it's little rewards. Sometimes, it's totally free rewards. Sometimes, it's food. And sometimes, it's turning writing into a game you can WIN!

And if there's anything I love more than rewards, it's WINNING!

~

Micro Rewards for Micro Progress

A lot of writers believe they should only get rewards for major accomplishments—selling a story to a pro-rate market, landing an agent, or getting nominated for an award (or winning an award).

But rewards don't have to be for major accomplishments. They can be for anything you want to reward yourself for.

Part of the trick is to scale the rewards appropriately, though. You probably shouldn't reward yourself with something massive every time you write 1,000 words, for example. Like the title of this section says: micro rewards for micro progress.

Here are some ideas.

~

Stickers

I love stickers. Stickers were a huge part of my grade school experience, and I always coveted the fancy ones I never had. When I realized as an adult, I can buy myself stickers, I absolutely did so. Now I have all the fancy stickers.

I mostly use my stickers as motivation combined with a record of what I've done. In my planner book,[1] if I get a thing done, I add a sticker. When I sell a story, I add a sticker. Sometimes, I have special stickers for special themes—a lot of my "sold a story" stickers have the word Yay on them, for example. When I'm doing a month-long writing challenge, I pull out a sheet of tiny stickers and use them to mark the days when I've done the challenge.

I'd have the stickers either way, but there's something about actually using them that works as a great form of motivation for me. Then I can look back at my planner book and see whether a week was productive or not, based on the number of stickers I've collected that week.

If you're writing a novel and want to use stickers as part of your rewards and/or motivation and to track your progress, choose some stickers and an arbitrary breakdown of the novel—maybe by word count, maybe by chapter, maybe on days when you work on

---

[1] Yes, I absolutely swear by a paper planner book. I could write pages upon pages about planner books and how they make my life better. Some people don't like planner books, but I say to them: where do you put your stickers?

the novel, whatever makes the most sense to you. Whether you have a paper planner or not, you should have a place to put the stickers—maybe a printout of a calendar or a blank sheet of paper, with or without a grid splitting your novel into those arbitrary categories above. Then, when you hit your goal, give yourself a sticker. And as the novel grows, so will your sheet of stickers!

~

Phone and Video Games

Another option is to reward yourself with a block of time when you get to do something you like, like playing a game on your phone or a video game. If you're using games as a motivator, be sure you set some limits around it, too. Like if you work for a couple of hours on your novel, then give yourself fifteen minutes of playing phone games or half an hour of playing a video game. You can scale these as appropriate to what you're playing—I know half an hour of a video game isn't always enough to accomplish something—but the goal is to spend more time writing than you spend playing a game. I know how easy it can be to get distracted with games on my phone, so I like to set a timer for myself, so I remember to get back to writing after my break.

Related to this is also buying yourself a game or a game-related treat. Most of the phone games I play have tons of built-in microtransactions, so spending a bit of money now and then to get some of the perks of the game could be a good reward. The same might go for a video game you want—maybe that's a reward for getting halfway through or done with your novel. It's easy for some of us to go overboard on this sort of thing, so do be careful about that, if you're prone to overspending on games.

~

TV Shows or Movies

This is another reward that can eat up time, so it's probably wise to use this one sparingly as well. But giving yourself half an hour to watch the latest episode of your favorite show, or something you've been streaming, can be a good small reward. Watching a movie is more of a time commitment, so it's better for a larger reward.

When I use TV shows or movies as rewards, I generally try to have them as the reward at the end of a day of working on writing, typically on the weekends. If I can get my to-do list done by dinner time, I'll reward myself with an episode (or three) of something I want to watch. But on the flip side, if I haven't finished my to-do list, then that's not a day I get that reward. It might seem harsh to place that limitation on myself, but for me, it works. (And also, there are days when I break this "rule," mostly when I've accomplished some things and need a break. I try not to make it a habit.)

~

Snacks

Snacks as a reward for writing get their own section. And while I firmly believe food should not be a reward, per se, there is a value in having specific foods set aside as treats for when you've reached a milestone. When I do NaNoWriMo, I almost always stock up on after-Halloween candy sales so I can have a small bit of candy when I hit my word count goal for the day.

One of my writer friends prefers Little Debbie Oatmeal Cream Pies, and I'd be right there with her if I could eat them. Stupid wheat. Another writer friend suggests pie in general, but unless you're also a baker (or buy pies at the store, I guess), that might be a slightly harder one to use as a regular reward. Maybe only for bigger milestones. (And again, with the stupid wheat, but at least my husband has a wonderful gluten-free pie crust recipe.)

Aside from snacks as rewards, eating while you write is an important thing to keep you fueled up. I'm surprisingly good at forgetting to eat, so having that reminder is valuable to me as well. Bodies need fuel, and until we can develop human photosynthesis (with appropriate UV protection), we're going to need to get fuel from food.

I suppose if you're using snacks as a reward, maybe they shouldn't all be sugar. This seems fake to me, because I have been known to fuel myself primarily on sugar, but it isn't a good idea. I guess. But as long as you're eating non-sugar too, a little sugar, as a treat, seems reasonable.

Also, while not a snack, I've been advised by my writer friends to include tea as a potential snack-related reward. Or maybe you should drink tea (if you like it) while you write. You could also pair tea with the idea of micro rewards, get yourself a tea sampler, and brew yourself a cup (or pot) when you hit exciting milestones.

~

Many Mini Prizes (a.k.a. the Advent Calendar Method)

I grew up Catholic, which meant we celebrated Advent—the four weeks leading up to Christmas. But Advent for us also meant an Advent Calendar. The main one we had was a cross-stitched "calendar" for the first twenty-five days of December, and each day had a ribbon so Mom could tie on a Hershey's Kiss. We had to take turns being the one who got the candy (because there were four kids), but it was our little countdown to Christmas.

Nowadays, you can get all sorts of Advent Calendars for the countdown from December 1 to 25. My niece and nephew got Lego Advent Calendars every year when they were younger. Some of my friends had a weird bootleg K-pop Advent Calendar a year or two ago. You can get them with stickers, wine, cheese, whiskey, whatever.

If you're not writing your novel in December (and, let's be honest, you're probably not, because writing a novel near the winter holidays is a disaster waiting to happen), you can still use a commercial Advent Calendar. Wait until about halfway through December, and those things are offered at a DEEP discount. So you can buy it in December but use it in whatever month you like. (Okay, maybe don't do that with the cheese one ...)

Alternately, you can make your own Advent Calendar, and it doesn't have to only have twenty-five days of rewards. You can figure out how you want to break up your novel, again, and then find the appropriate number of rewards for that division. Then you can hit up a dollar store or bargain bins for sufficient "prizes" for your own writing Advent Calendar. And you can also buy bigger rewards for the bigger goals.

~

Bigger Rewards for Bigger Goals

Of course, all your rewards don't have to be micro, because not all of your goals are micro. You're allowed to give yourself bigger rewards for hitting bigger goals. One author who was working on a novel wrapped up ten presents, each one to correspond with the completion of 10,000 words of a novel. In this author's case, most of the presents were food, beverages, or things that smell nice, with a bottle of Prosecco as the 100,000-word reward.

You don't have to go this identical route. Maybe your smaller presents will be stickers, pens, and notebooks, and your big reward will be a fancy pen or notebook. Maybe you'll use small blocks of time on a video game for your smaller rewards, and then buy yourself the video game you've been dreaming of when you finish the novel.

For me, I find with this method, I have to give myself the promise of "I will get this thing when I get to this word count" but not actually BUY the thing until I've done that. I convinced myself with one novel I should buy myself the reward for finishing it in advance, and that reward is now in a box on my shelf, and the novel isn't done (nor will it probably ever be). If you're like me, making yourself wait to make the purchase might be a better motivator, because if you've already bought all the things, what's to stop you from opening them early?

~

Free Rewards

Sometimes, you don't have the money to spend on rewards for yourself. And while a couple of the rewards I talked about earlier might be viable in that case, I've also got suggestions for rewards that cost you zero dollars and zero cents.

~

Social Media Brag Posts

Sometimes, your reward can be accolades other people give you, whether those come in the form of likes, boosts, toots, or whatever we're calling the latest "like" function on the social media platform of your choosing.

When you hit a milestone in your novel writing, post about it to social media. It costs no money, and it's likely other people will react positively to it, which then gives you happy feelings. And it can be the reward that keeps on giving, as you rack up more likes or hearts or whatever.

Some people may ignore your brag posts, and the mighty algorithm on many platforms means some people might not see them at all, but if you're looking for a way to celebrate and reward yourself, brag posts are one way to go.

~

Naps

I'm going to begin by saying I hate naps. As I famously told my husband after one nap, "They make me feel like I've been covered in dirt." We aren't sure if this was Sleepy Me's way of saying "buried alive" or "gross," but either way, I stand by it. Napping doesn't make me feel more rested or better.

But I'm an outlier, and I know it. Other people love naps. And if you're one of those people, sometimes, a nap is its own reward. So if you like naps, and if you've reached a milestone in your writing, take a nap. Go wild! Only not too wild, because a) you're napping and b) you probably shouldn't use finishing some writing as a reason to go to bed at like 2 p.m. Unless that's your normal bedtime.

The potential added bonus of a nap as a reward is if you dream when you nap, it might count as brainstorming. This might also mean a nap could be a distraction that's also a tool. But the flip side is a nap could be just a distraction. So reward yourself with naps if you like, or use them to get some brainstorming in, but make sure they don't become a distraction instead of a reward or tool.

~

Long (or Short) Walks (on the Beach or Otherwise)

Got some writing done? Take a walk.

Not everyone thinks of a walk as a reward, but they certainly can be if you enjoy walking. If you want to make the reward extra special, you could take a walk somewhere different than your own neighborhood, though that might involve driving or using transit, which are probably not entirely free.

Taking a walk as a reward has the added benefit of being good for your body. And because sitting at a computer and typing all day can be bad for your body, it's nice to be able to counteract that somewhat by doing something that's good for you. (Arguably, taking a break to do some stretches could also be a reward, but maybe that's something writers should be doing anyway.)

Taking a walk or doing some other kind of physical activity can also be good for brainstorming or working through story problems. So again, this one falls into the category of maybe a distraction that is also a tool.

Taking a walk outside isn't viable for everyone. If you've got mobility issues or another form of physical disability, it could be difficult or impossible to go for a walk. If you live in a place where it's not safe to walk around outside, due to traffic, crime, or other factors, I similarly don't recommend it. And if you're writing late at night and it's pitch black outside when you're ready for a reward, it might not be advisable to go for a walk, again for safety reasons, and also because who wants to stumble around in the dark?

If you find yourself in one of these situations, an alternative is to find videos on YouTube (or similar platforms) of people taking walks in their neighborhoods. These might also count as research, if you're writing something set in a location you don't live in and/or have never been to. The downside of these videos is it's easy to get sucked into the rabbit hole of a video site that recommends what you should watch next. But as long as you limit your time and don't let this turn into a distraction, it's a reasonable way to "walk" without leaving your house. (It doesn't give you the physical benefits, of course, unless you have a treadmill and set up the video on some device, so it seems like you're walking in the location of the video. I guess you could also pace around your living space if you don't have a treadmill. Or march in place like my mom does when her activity tracker tells her she needs to move.)

~

Don't Let Rewards Turn into Distractions

I've mentioned a handful of things that could be rewards and also become distractions. And sometimes, they wind up bleeding into each other. So while it's important to give yourself rewards for your accomplishments, you need to be conscious of how much time those rewards might eat up.

I've often got many tabs open when I'm writing, some of which are for research, but others of which are social media or online writing communities or browser games. It's always a peril when I switch from my writing software to my browser, because even if I'm ostensibly going there to look at some research or look something up, I get distracted by the shiny. If there's an alert on one of my online writing communities, I'll go check that out. And then twenty minutes have passed, and I don't remember what I needed to look up.

Some people have a lot more discipline than I do, and they can ignore (or close!) those other tabs when they need to focus on writing. They're probably safe from letting their rewards turn into distractions.

But if you're like me, you might need something more to keep you on track. Timers work well for me. Other writers swear by browser plug-ins that keep you from accessing certain sites during certain times of the day. Some people turn off their Wi-Fi while they write. (That idea terrifies me. How can you do random bits of research without Wi-Fi?!)

Whatever it takes to make sure your rewards don't turn into distractions is valid, so long as it works for you. Sometimes, being aware of the danger is enough. When it's not, use other tricks.

~

Gamifying Your Writing

Gamification is defined as "the application of typical elements of game playing (e.g. point scoring, competition with others, rules of play) to other areas of activity, typically as an online marketing technique to encourage engagement with a product or service." In addition to the marketing applications, for some writers, gamifying writing tasks can be a great motivator, as it helps you celebrate small wins to encourage you to keep going.

There are tons of websites that will help you to gamify your writing by offering you fancy charts and graphs, pictures of cats, cute avatars, or experience points for a little virtual character. It's impossible to say what sites will or will not be available at the time you're reading this. If you search for "gamifying writing" or "writing gamification" (what a word!), you'll probably find a lot of articles on the subject, but some of those will mention where you can find these games or apps.

However, you don't need to use a fancy website to gamify your writing. You can use some of the same techniques of setting milestones and giving yourself rewards as your version of gamification. What the websites do have, though, is a level of accountability and a different sense of accomplishment. And for some people, that's a much better motivator than other rewards.

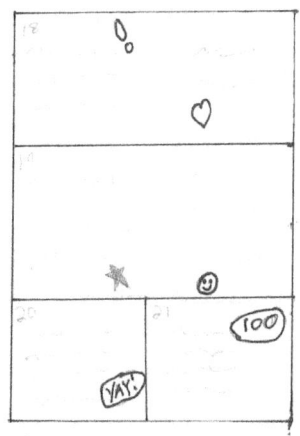

My own form of gamifying my writing is stickers (yes, again). I use stickers in my planner book to mark days when I've hit my word count goal (when I have those), days when I've worked on a non-word project (but still writing related, like editing), when I complete a new story or poem, and when I sell a story or poem. If I'm feeling discouraged about my writing, I can flip back through the previous weeks and see what I've accomplished. And if those pages are looking a bit boring and devoid of stickers, I can use that as motivation to do a thing that lets me add a sticker to the current day.

CONCLUSION

Writing is hard. As such, writing novels is hard. It will take a lot of your time, quite likely much more than you think. And you may take all that time, get to the end, and realize you don't like your own novel.

(If you get to that point, DO NOT delete everything you've written. Put it away. Give it some space. Come back to it later. It may not be quite as bad as you think. We are our own worst critics, after all.)

But is it worth it to write a novel anyway, knowing all this?

Your mileage may vary. But if you've read this whole book, you're certainly thinking about writing a novel, if you haven't already begun. I think it's worth it to give it a shot. You may discover, like I have, that writing novels isn't for you. But you can try it out, which is an important step in making that decision.

Or you may decide, like many other authors, that the novel length and format is exactly what you want to be writing for the rest of your days.

In either case, congratulations! Whether you try and say no or try and say yes, you will have written a novel! That's a whole lot of words, a whole lot of work, and a whole lot of time. And it's a major accomplishment. Celebrate that, even before you think about the remainder of the process of getting said novel out into the world.

Then take a nap, have some tea, or whatever you prefer, so you can come back to your work refreshed!

APPENDIX: COMMERCIAL IDEA DECKS

I've accumulated a collection of commercial idea decks of cards (and one with dice). Different decks in this list provide different types of ideas, so be sure to look at the types of ideas you hope to find!

There are a few decks I own that are not available as of this writing, so I haven't included those here. There is always a possibility others will go out of print in the future. I apologize in advance if that is the case!

Characters

Reckless Deck: Cards to inspire a character. This set is meant as art prompts, but I often use art prompts for writing prompts, and this deck works for either. Includes fantasy, sci-fi, horror, and steampunk genres, plus add-ons for subgenres. You can use these cards to come up with a random character or to add additional characteristics to an existing character.

https://recklessdeck.com[1]

Reckless Deck Apprentice Pack: Kid-friendly cards to inspire a character. While the main Reckless Deck is not unfriendly to kids, the Apprentice Pack is specifically geared toward kids. The

---

[1] Reckless Deck also has an expansion called Psyche, which should be out in 2024. This has been a long-delayed project, but it expands the options for character-related ideas.

Wonderland Expansion to the Apprentice Pack is entirely Alice in Wonderland themed. Similar to the main Reckless deck, you can use these cards to come up with a random character or to add additional characteristics to an existing character.

https://recklessdeck.com/collections/decks/products/the-apprentice-pack

Plot

Story Engine: Cards to help you develop a plot. You lay out five cards, one of each type (Agents, Engines, Anchors, Conflicts, and Aspects), and put them together to create a plot, with two or four options on each card to choose from. There are many, many genre-specific expansions, mostly revolving around fantasy, sci-fi, and horror. You can use these cards to create plots and subplots, ranging from huge plots for a series down to small plots for short fiction.

https://storyenginedeck.com/ [2]

Worldbuilding

Reckless Deck Worlds: Cards for worldbuilding. Similar to the core Reckless deck, this is meant as art prompts but for creating a world. Includes information on how to use specific categories (excluding others) to make the worldbuilding work for a low technology setting. You can use these cards for worldbuilding or potentially for story seeds.

https://recklessdeck.com/collections/decks/products/reckless-deck-worlds

Multi-Function

Decuma: Cards that ask questions. Designed as a gaming tool to help with collaborative worldbuilding, location details,

---

[2] Story Engine also has the Deck of Worlds, which is one of the few decks I don't have, but it's a worldbuilding deck. They are also releasing the Lore Master's Deck in 2024 for more plot-related options!

connections between characters, and setting conflicts, this also works for writers who want inspiration on similar things. As such, you can use these cards to create a world or detail portions of that world, create character relationships, and generate plot ideas.

https://goldenlassogames.com/pages/decuma

Publishing Goblin's Oracle Dice (and cards): Dice and cards for fortune telling. Though this set is closer to a tarot set, with a complex system related to the dice, there are aspects that can be used for writing ideas. You can use these cards and dice to create a plot element or characters, though both involve a significant amount of randomness.

https://publishinggoblin.com/products/divination/oracle-dice-2nd-ed/

Story Forge: Cards to help get you unstuck. You lay out spreads similar to tarot spreads, and whether the cards are upright or "reversed" makes a difference. You can use these cards to create an entire plot, for inspiration on what comes next in a plot, or to develop characters with backstory and motivations.

http://storyforgecards.com/

Writer Emergency Pack: Cards to help you get unstuck or outline. While the basic idea of this deck is to help you get unstuck when you don't know what should happen next in a story or novel, I also see this as being useful when you're outlining a novel (or story) and get stuck or want to inject something unexpected. Each card presents multiple options and art that can also inspire other options. (There are two different versions of this deck; the XL version has more options on each card.) You can use these cards to get unstuck while writing or plotting.

https://writeremergency.com/

ABOUT THE AUTHOR

Dawn Vogel has written for children, teens, and adults, spanning genres, places, and time periods. More than 100 of her stories and poems have been published by small and large presses. Her specialties include young protagonists, siblings who bicker but love each other in the end, and things in the water that want you dead. She is a member of Broad Universe, SFWA, and Codex Writers. She lives in Seattle with her awesome husband (and fellow author), Jeremy Zimmerman, and their herd of cats. Visit her at historythatneverwas.com or on BlueSky @historyneverwas.